Daggers & Donuts

Paranormal Cozy Mystery

B I Skinner

Contents

Chapter 1

"Hey, lady!" Marshall and Marcus, my rabbit familiars, shout at me. They're actually my Gran's familiars, who I inherited when she passed away. For some reason, when they start a sentence with "Hey lady," it's often a precursor of bad news.

"Hey, rabbits," I respond. "Don't tell me you found another body."

Marcus, the leader of the two, shrugs his tiny rabbit shoulders. "Okay," he says as they start to hop off.

"Wait!" I call after them. "I was kidding. You didn't really find a body, did you?"

Last spring, Stumpy the cat found a body in a nearby park. Now amid the Crested Peaks 4th of July celebration, it appears that the rabbits are telling me there's yet another dead body. How does this keep happening?

"I suppose she could be taking a nap behind the tent," Marshall offers.

This doesn't sound good at all.

"Who could be taking a nap behind what tent?" I ask. I refuse to wrap my head around the idea that one of my familiars has discovered another untimely death.

"The sparkly lady who's lying on the ground behind the magician's tent," Marshall explains.

"Perhaps she's practicing a magic trick?" I offer.

"Sure, if you say so," says Marcus as they turn to leave again.

I raise my hand. "Wait! Why don't you show me?"

I'll humor them. I consider asking Detective Drew Bailey, with the Crested Peaks Police Department, who also happens to be my boyfriend, to come with us. He's several booths down, drinking a beer, and joking with one of his friends, but I decide against it. What are the odds that they've actually found another body?

I fall in behind the rabbits as they saunter in the direction of the magician's tent. After my Gran died, in addition to her rabbits, I inherited her vegetarian breakfast café called Marcall's. Yes, she named the restaurant after the rabbits.

I'm the only one who can communicate with them - aside from Stumpy the cat - who they invited to come live with us without consulting me first. Now before this sounds too weird, Stumpy doesn't talk to me; he talks to the rabbits, who then pass on what he said. Nope, it's not weird at all.

On our way to this supposed body, it hits me. "Did you say the lady was sparkly?"

"Yep!"

"Why did you say that?"

"Because she glitters in the sun," Marcus persists.

Now I'm sure they don't know what they're talking about. I mean, who sparkles? "Where's Stumpy, by the way?" When Stumpy found a body in the park the three of them came to the cafe to tell me.

"Last time I saw him, he was chasing a grasshopper near the dunk tank," Marshall tells me.

As we approach the magician's tent, I'm relieved that I don't see anything unusual. "I don't see anything, you guys. Are you sure you weren't just imagining it?"

"Sparkly lady is around back," Marshall says as he and Marcus look at each other like I'm just too dumb to understand anything. They do that a lot. My grandma always claimed to have won them in a poker game. But that was decades ago, so no one is sure just how old they are.

Gran was the only one who could communicate with them until she died last summer, and then somehow, the ability transferred to me. They don't have magical powers like I do. They mostly just run around town scamming treats from people.

They're orange and white with helicopter ears. My Gran liked to say they look like Colby cheese. I'm impressed with the way they get around the town, given their size. They only weigh about four pounds each, but they seem to cover a large distance throughout Crested Peaks.

As we walk between the magician's tent and the one next to it, I'm dismayed to see a large object glinting in the sun. When we get closer, I realize it's the rhinestone-studded costume of the magician's assistant I saw perform at a show recently.

I run to her side, but the dagger in her chest tells me there's nothing I can do for her. Fear grips me as I realize there is indeed a body here, and I just found it. Again. I know I need to get Drew over here right away, but first, I lean over her to get a better look.

My pulse quickens as I peer at her pale face. I start to back up when a blood-curdling scream reverberates off the surrounding tents. I'm so startled I jump back, and the rabbits take off across the park like they've been shot from a cannon. A woman is staring at the body in horror as she screams and points at me.

"Shhhh!" I tell her because I can't think of anything better to say, and I just want her to stop screaming.

Chapter 2

The noise draws a small crowd, and as others see the body, they shout and gasp in shock. I'm rooted to the spot while I continue to stand over the lifeless corpse. When Drew and two police officers round the corner to see what the commotion is about, the screaming woman pauses, takes a deep breath, points at me, and shouts, "She did it! I saw her!"

Trust me when I say Drew does not look happy to see me here.

"Charlotte! What are you doing here? What's going on?"

"Uhhhhh," is the most brilliant thing I can think to say at the moment.

"Secure the area!" Drew barks at the men with him. The officers quickly work to push the crowd back. One of them calls on his radio for barriers and yellow tape.

Drew rushes to my side, guiding me away from the growing crowd, his hand gently tugging my elbow. "What happened, Char?" Concern, as well as frustration, etches his ruggedly handsome face.

As I stare up into his deep emerald eyes, which are full of worry, I know he's tired of finding me at crime scenes. I speak softly, so no one overhears us, "I don't know! Marshall and Marcus came to get me. They told me they saw a body at the magician's tent."

Drew sighs loudly. He's one of the few people who know that the rabbits talk to me. And yes, that was a super fun conversation. Everybody knows I'm a witch, but not everyone would understand about the rabbit familiars.

In a town like Crested Peaks, where Supernatural beings live openly with Non Supernatural beings, a witch is not that unusual. Enchanted rabbits, however, are an entirely different story

"When did they tell you this?" he asks.

"Not even ten minutes ago. They came up to me and said they found a body that sparkled."

Drew glances back at the body on the ground. "Rhinestones," he mutters.

"Yes. So, I followed them, hoping they were mistaken."

"Why didn't you give me a head's up? I was a few feet away."

"I told you. I was sure they were mistaken. What are the odds of them finding another body?"

"Pretty good from the looks of it," he responds grimly. "But what am I supposed to tell my captain about how you found the body? I obviously can't tell him your talking rabbits lead you to it."

"I don't know," I sigh. "Tell him I was out walking and accidentally stumbled across it."

The woman who had been screaming was giving her statement to the police. She keeps glaring at me accusingly. Great. Who knows what she's telling them?

"Walk me through this. What happened once you got here? Was the victim already like this?"

I glare at him. "No, she was just standing here, minding her own business, until I stabbed her," I retort.

Now he's even more frustrated. "I meant did you touch anything. Did you move the body at all? Obviously, you didn't stab her!"

People are watching us argue with growing interest. I hope they don't think there's anything suspicious happening. In a small town like Crested Peaks, nearly all the locals know that I'm dating a detective.

They also know that this is the fourth body I've come across in less than a year. I wouldn't want to get Drew in trouble and make it look like he was playing favorites. Given that I'm often in trouble with him for investigating things on my own anyway.

"I swear I didn't touch a thing. We walked up, and I saw her. I moved closer to get a better look, saw the dagger in her chest, and then that woman saw us and screamed. Scared the heck out of the rabbits and me. The rabbits took off across the park."

"Did you see or hear anything unusual?"

"No."

"Which direction did you come from?"

I point between the two tents. "We cut through there."

Just then, we hear a shout, "No Darla! No! No!" as Harold, the magician, sprints between the opposite side of the tents and straight for his assistant's body. It takes two police officers to hold him back; he's thrashing around so hard and wailing.

"How did this happen? Who did this?" he cries while the officers pull him to the side.

Last spring, while I was held at gunpoint by a mob kingpin, I experienced a surge of energy I'd never encountered before. A sense of profound knowing swept through my body while every nerve ending felt like it was tingling and crackling.

It's hard to describe it even now, and believe me, I've tried over and over since then to accurately label the sensation. I just knew that she was going to fire the gun on the FBI agent who was trying to help me. I wasn't reading her mind or anything, but I just knew.

And now, watching Harold, I have a similar feeling of knowing something. Yet, I can't pinpoint exactly what it is. I just know without a doubt he has a secret he doesn't want anyone to know about. I'm horrified. Did he kill his assistant? Is this grief all an act?

'No!"/Drew says so sharply I jump. I stare back at him, wondering what that's all about.

"I. Know. That. Look. By. Now." he says very pointedly. "Don't even think about getting involved in this."

"I was just watching him react to his assistant's murder," I explain innocently.

"I know how you are, Charlotte. Stay out of this and let the police handle it."

"Okay. Okay," I mutter as I hold my hands up in surrender. He glowers at me because neither one of us believes me.

"You should get back to your booth while we work on things here. I'll contact you if we need anything more."

"As my boyfriend, I assume you'll be contacting me later, regardless?" I remind him.

"Yes, of course," he responds with a distracted look back. Drew is dedicated to his job and sometimes forgets things like eating, sleeping, and calling his girlfriend.

But I head back to the booth we rented for the festival anyway. By now, I've learned to recognize when he's in the zone, and I'll just be in his way if I stick around.

Chapter 3

We sold Damien's famous and outrageously delicious black bean breakfast burritos. In addition to some quadruple berry smoothies, which I mixed up myself using a little witchcraft. It's a concoction made of blueberries, raspberries, goji berries, and strawberries with just a hint of almond extract. The berries, and a drop of magic, help boost the immune system. In addition to being delicious, of course.

As I approach the booth, Damien, Marcall's height-challenged but brilliant chef, and Miranda, my best friend and witching mentor, run to greet me. I notice that Miranda has colored her spiky hair red, white and blue for the occasion.

"What happened? Are you okay? Is there really a body over there? Did you see it?" They fire questions at me in rapid succession without letting me answer.

"We tried to get back there, but the police wouldn't let us! What's going on?" Damien asks.

I sigh loudly as I start to grasp that there's a dead woman not far from here. "The rabbits found a body and came to get me."

"Again?" Damien unhelpfully reminds me.

"Do you know how she died?" Miranda asks.

"I'd say the dagger in her chest is a good sign."

Miranda gasps, clasping her hand over her mouth while Damien cringes and shakes his head.

"That's horrible. Who would do such a thing?" Miranda cries.

"Is it anybody we know?" Damien asks.

"It looked like it was Darla, the magician's assistant. I never met her, but I saw her perform at a show recently," I tell them.

When all the color drains from Damien's face, I know something is terribly wrong. "Are you sure it was Darla?" he asks.

"It certainly looked like her, and when Harold the magician showed up, he screamed Darla when he saw her. Why did you know her?"

"She's my cousin Cody's girlfriend," Damien whispers.

"Oh, that's awful." I lay my hand on Damien's arm for support because I don't know what else to do at this point. "I'm not even sure what to say. Do you need to leave? I can take care of things here; you should go be with your family."

"But I don't want to leave you here to handle this all by yourself."

Damien's husband Tom steps up. "I'll stay and help Charlotte finish, and then I'll meet up with you afterward. Will that work?"

I nod my head at him, "That's a great idea. You go and be with your family right now, and Tom and I will pack things up and take them back to the café. I have a feeling the festival will be winding down now anyway."

"Thanks, I appreciate it. I think I'll run over to my mom's house first. She should hear this from me."

I give my chef and dear friend a quick hug and send him on his way. What a horrible way to end the festival. Damien was Marcall's chef while my Gran was still alive, and I'm incredibly grateful he chose to stay on even after she passed.

He's not only a gifted chef but he's also become one of my dearest friends. He's the cautious one who tries his best to keep Miranda and me in line. It rarely works, but he definitely tries.

I glance over at Tom as he begins to gather up the leftover napkins. "When the rabbits said she was sparkly, I didn't understand what they meant at first. That's also why I hoped they were wrong.

"But when we got there, she was lying on the ground on her back, with the dagger sticking out of her chest. And she was still wearing her performance costume. Sparkling in the sunlight."

Tom lets out a low whistle, "That makes what, the fourth body you've found in a year? The fourth you've found since you've been back in Crested Peaks, right? People must be starting to won—"

He stops short when he sees Miranda make slashing motions across her throat, and when he turns to find me scowling at him, his cheeks turn pink. "Oops, sorry about that. I talk too much when I'm upset. I just can't believe this happened to someone I know."

"It looks I was right. The surest way to clear out a festival is a dead body," I point out as the three of us scan the area noting how empty everything suddenly got.

"What should we do with the leftovers," Tom asks. "I hate to just waste it."

I point to the First Aid tent. "Let's give it to them." Tom quickly boxes up the leftovers and heads over to the tent where the nurses and EMTs volunteer to help revelers suffering from heatstroke or bee stings.

They're thrilled to get the breakfast burritos and smoothies, and I make a note to offer free food to first responders at events from now on. We pack up the remainder of our things and get ready to head back to the café.

Bubbles, Tom and Damien's rescued Pibble, trots along at my side cheerfully. She's wearing a festive red, white, and blue bow today. She's such a happy dog who loves everyone and always looks like she's smiling. Marshall, Marcus, and Stumpy are sitting atop the supplies packed in the wagon, waiting to be wheeled home.

All three of them give Bubbles the evil eye. "Does she talk to you?" I ask. I've been wondering about that for a while but haven't asked until now.

Tom looks up at me sharply. He knows that even though Damien is used to the paranormal activity, for which Crested Peaks is well known, there's just something about the talking rabbits that makes him nervous. He'd really freak if his dog could talk.

"Nope!" says Marcus. "That's the creepy part. She doesn't say a word. Just sits there with that ridiculous grin on her face and drooling. It's unnatural if you ask me."

I laugh. "A dog that doesn't talk is unnatural. Of course." Stumpy looks down at her from his lofty perch swishing his tail angrily.

I wave at Miranda, whose coffee shop is several booths down, to let her know we're leaving. Tom pulls the wagon while Marshall, Marcus, and Stumpy ride along as if they just naturally expect others to cater to their every need. Meanwhile, Bubbles keeps up her stride along with us, not a care in the world.

When we arrive back at the cafe, Gladys, the town gossip, is out front chatting with a friend. Gladys has all the tea, all the time, and prides herself on it. If you need information, she's the one to consult.

A few months ago, she discovered that two famous reality TV stars were hiding out in a cabin nearby. But the surprise was they weren't the two who were supposed to be together.

As far as the rest of the world knew, the star of the show was happily engaged to the winner. Gladys, however, broke the news that he wasn't with the first-place winner, but the woman who came in fourth place instead!

Damien and I were so shocked when they showed up at Marcall's the day before our Easter celebration that we could barely talk. TMZ has nothing on Gladys.

She's a tall, thin woman with a shock of fuzzy gray hair who always dresses impeccably. Today she's dressed for the festivities with linen shorts, a red blouse, and a red, white, and blue scarf knotted at her throat.

Her navy-blue straw hat is perched jauntily on her head. "Good morning, Gladys!" I call out to her while Tom lets himself into the restaurant to unload the supplies.

"Oh, thank goodness you're back!" she cries. "I've just heard the most dreadful news! Darla Wagner, the magician's assistant, was found murdered in the park at the festival."

"It's true," I confirm.

"I've also heard that she was riddled with machine-gun bullets."

"Uh, no, that's not true." I'm not sure how much I should let on at this point. I don't want to mess up Drew's investigation or anything, but I doubt there's harm in pointing out that she was not gunned down in a hail of bullets.

"But you're the one who first discovered the body?"

"Regretfully, yes. Well, technically, it was the rabbits, but they just showed me where to find her."

"There's been some talk that when Harold hired her as his assistant, it's because something was going on between them, if you know what I mean," Gladys tsks.

"Really? Isn't she a little young for him?"

"Young and naive! It's not like she had experience in that line of work either. She was waiting tables at Denny's when he hired her. They tell me that Hilda Barnes, his girlfriend, was furious. She'd taken to following the poor girl around town thinking she might catch them in the act."

I ponder the news for a moment. "That would give Hilda motive to kill, wouldn't it?"

Gladys nods her head vigorously. "It would certainly give me motive to kill!" she growls as she mimics shooting someone.

"Gladys!" I exclaim. I can't decide if I should be scared about this or laugh at her theatrics.

"That's what would happen if I had ever caught my dear Barney; God rest his soul, messing around with some young chippy behind my back."

"I can't imagine that your late husband ever even considered it for a second," I reassure her.

Once again, for good measure, she makes shooting gestures with her fingers. Yikes.

After I've sent Gladys and her finger guns on her way, I help Tom put everything back.

"You know you don't have to help me put all of this away. You can go to Damien now if you want."

Tom shakes his head. "He just texted and said he's with his mom at his aunt's house, and it's all very chaotic and that I should just stay here and help you."

"If you're sure."

"Trust me, I'm sure. Damien wouldn't tell me to stay here if he didn't mean it. He also said to tell you that you're still supposed to go to the fireworks show tonight."

My mouth drops. How did he know exactly what I was thinking?

Tom smiles in answer to my thoughts. "Because he knows how you are and knew that the first thing you'd offer to do is come right over and help out. But he also remembered that this is your first time entering the fireworks display contest, and he insists that you be there for the show."

"You picked a great guy Tom."

He beams at me. "I know."

"Tell him that the moment he needs anything, I'll be there."

Tom nods. "I will tell him that, and I assure you, he already knows it as well.

After we finish up at the cafe, Tom and Bubbles get ready to head home while I do the same with my own furry companions.

I can't stop thinking about Damien's cousin and what he must be going through. To have your girlfriend stabbed to death in broad daylight, in the middle of a festival even, is so harsh. I can't even begin to understand it.

But then I feel guilty thinking about this evening's events. I was really looking forward to the entire thing. A picnic with all my friends and then the fireworks show. Crested Peaks is beginning to feel like the first solid home I've ever had, despite the close calls I've had with crazed criminals. I

It's so different from New York City in every way. And yes, I lived here as a teenager, but the only thing I saw back then was my own angst as an orphan. Now, I purposely take time to do things like sip tea while reading a book, on the wrap around porch of my grandma's house. I stare up in awe at the jagged mountain edges that surrounding the entire community and I wonder how I never noticed this before.

I also failed to appreciate how the community really cares for and looks out for each other. I know my neighbors' names, and they know mine. When I come home from work in the winter, after a long day at the café, I often find that someone has shoveled my sidewalk for me.

The friends that I've made working at the café have become the family I never had. Their loyalty is fierce, and I love them for it. And now my heart breaks for what Damien's family must be going through. Darla's family too. I don't know them, but I can't imagine losing someone so young in such a violent way.

I'm in a somber mood as I climb the steps to my home, the home my grandmother left me. Still, when the rabbits and Stumpy all scramble up the steps beside me, racing for the door in a competition to see who gets there first, I can't help but laugh. The three of them are the most entertaining creatures I could have imagined. And even though Marshall and Marcus basically adopted Stumpy without telling me I'm glad they did.

I just never imagined, when I returned to Crested Peaks, that I'd live with three dead body finding, crime-solving, talking fur balls.

Chapter 4

I feed the boys an early dinner, which they all happily inhale, and then pass out for a quick nap before leaving for the fireworks and picnic event at the Hotel Glacier. When the rabbits invited a newly homeless Stumpy to move in with us a few months ago, they did it without bothering to even ask me first.

He followed us out to the car after closing the cafe one evening. When I asked what he was doing, the rabbits said they told him he could live with us because the new tenant next door, where he had lived for years, threatened to take him to the shelter if he didn't leave.

He's a gray tabby cat who has stumps for back legs. He claims he's a war veteran. As much as I'd like to doubt that, once upon a time, I didn't believe in talking animals either, so who knows.

I haven't heard from Drew since we left the festival, which doesn't surprise me. There's a reason he made detective within only a few years of joining the force, even though it's almost unheard of. So, when

Miranda texts me to see if I want to ride to the fireworks show with her and her boyfriend Miles, the town librarian, I quickly agree.

I'm eager to discuss what seems to be the latest Crested Peaks murder, as well as what I sensed with Harold, the magician. I text Drew to let him know I'm riding to the hotel with Miranda, and I'm relieved when he writes back to say he'll meet us there later. I was worried he might end up canceling altogether.

The fireworks show in Crested Peaks is unique because the displays are artfully designed by witches and wizards, and there's a competition involved for the best display. Miranda won last year. And while her display this year is mostly a secret, from what little she's told me, I bet she'll win again.

Since this is my first year designing a display, mine is pretty basic, but I'm still excited about it. We don't do traditional fireworks shows here because we're in the mountains, and the pine trees could catch fire if a stray spark landed somewhere it shouldn't. Another special part about our show is that it's mostly silent, with no booming noises, so it's pet and veteran friendly.

Some of the experienced Supernaturals, like Miranda, include music with their display, but I'm not that adept yet. Each display is limited to 60 seconds. They had to implement that rule because one year, a wizard produced a three-hour show, and everyone else got bored and went home.

The event is held behind the Hotel Glacier, overlooking the lake, with the picturesque mountains as a backdrop. Harvey, one of our favorite ghosts who lives at the hotel, gets especially excited because it's one of the town events he can actually attend. He was killed at a shootout in the hotel in the late 1800s which made it his permanent home.

He's been very helpful with solving the last two murders because being at the most popular hotel in town, he sees a lot of people come and go. And as a ghost, he can move around the huge and elaborate hotel, undetected, when he wants to.

Once Miranda and Miles arrive at my house, Miles takes the picnic basket from me to load in their car. He busies himself trying to talk to the rabbits and Stumpy. He's fascinated by the fact I can communicate with them, and he's always hoping somehow they'll slip up and say something to him.

Miranda is my amazing magic mentor. My parents were Supernaturals, who also happened to be con artists, that were killed over a deal gone wrong, and that's when I was sent to live with Gran. As a teenager, I chose to deny my magical abilities, so I wouldn't turn out like my parents. After high school, I moved to New York City, hoping to escape my past.

Thankfully, however, when I moved back to Crested Peaks, I realized it wasn't the magic that made my parents crooks; it was just my parents' period. But after more than two decades of refusing to develop my craft, I sorely needed proper training and a ton of practice. Miranda has been a huge help with that.

"Heard anything from Drew?" Miranda asks.

"He's busy with the case, but he'll meet us at the hotel as soon as he can."

"What about Damien?" she asks, shaking her head in disbelief.

"Tom insisted we aren't needed at this time. Damien texted later and insisted that we enjoy ourselves at the picnic. He said that there will be plenty of time tomorrow for us to fuss over him and his family." I respond.

"I can't imagine what they must be going through."

"I was thinking the exact same thing earlier. I still feel a little guilty for going to the events tonight, but Damien says it's so chaotic at his aunt's house right now we would just be in the way as it is."

"I'm sure he'll let us know when he's ready."

"By the way, there is something I want to ask you about."

"Of course," Miranda replies.

"When Harold saw Darla's body, he was distraught. Like over the top upset, which seemed odd for someone who's just her boss. But that wasn't the really weird part. I felt the same overwhelming and electrifying energy that I did when The Jackal was holding me at gunpoint. I'm still struggling to make sense of it."

"Like a gut feeling?" Miles asks.

"It's so much more than that. It's more like an energy. It's just something that I know. Without a doubt. Like with The Jackal. I knew she was about to pull the trigger and that I had to act fast."

"And that's when you used magic to hit her with the whiskey bottle and deflect the gun," Miranda reminds us.

"Yeah," I respond softly.

"As you know, there are some Supernaturals who are pure psychics, and there are empaths too. But my guess is, as a witch, you also have inherited some form of psychic ability."

"That's exciting and scary all at once," I point out.

"Indeed, it is," Miranda responds.

"Did your grandma have psychic abilities?" Miles asks.

I shake my head regretfully, "I don't know. She never mentioned it, and I never noticed it. And here's another question, why didn't I get that same feeling when Bryce held me at gunpoint?"

Miranda pauses thoughtfully. "When you first came back to Crested Peaks, you were just beginning to acknowledge you're a witch. I suspect that as you practice and accept your powers on a deeper level;

you'll not only gain and polish skills, your natural abilities will be heightened as well."

"How many times have you been held at gunpoint?" Miles asks.

"Too many!" Miranda and I answer in unison.

When we arrive at the fireworks picnic, it looks like the entire town is here. Marshall, Marcus, and Stumpy all run off through the crowd in search of their friends and to beg treats from as many people as possible. Miranda, Miles, and I snag a prime spot right next to a 100-year-old maple tree.

"How is it with so many people here, this spot isn't taken? This is the best spot in the area!"

Miranda giggles.

"What?" I ask her.

Miles leans over to whisper to me. "She does this every year - she bewitches the spot to look like there's a big, noisy family already sitting here. The Supernaturals know it's bewitched, and anybody who isn't invited by Miranda who tries to sit here develops a sudden case of poison ivy rash. The Non Supernaturals see a large and boisterous family in this spot and move on."

"How come I don't think of things like that?" I ask.

"Stick with me kid, you will eventually!" Miranda laughs.

We lay out the blanket and unpack the picnic basket while I text Drew to let him know where we are.

He texts back:

Under the usual tree?

How did you know?

Miranda manages to snag that spot every year for some reason.

"Are you nervous about your first magical fireworks display?" Miranda interrupts our texting.

"A little. Although, as you know, it's pretty basic. Nothing fancy."

"Everyone will love it, I'm sure."

"What about your display?"

"Oh, I'm more than ready. And Penelope Fishbea won't know what hit her."

I look at Miles in confusion. This is the first I've heard this name.

"Penelope Fishbea is Miranda's magical arch nemesis."

Miranda screws up her face. "She's a hack! And a cheater! And she beat me twice in the last five years. And whenever she does beat me, she spends the year rubbing it in my face."

"The nerve!" I exclaim in mock offense.

"Right? I swear she has spies out there just hoping to catch a glimpse of what I'm working on. I have to be so top secret about the whole thing."

I shrug my shoulders at Miles, "Even I know very little about her display."

"She doesn't tell me either," he says.

"You can never be too careful," Miranda grumbles.

I'm extra happy to see Drew walk toward us a few minutes later. "Hey everybody!" he calls out, carrying a bottle of wine and a fresh baguette from our favorite bakery.

Miles jumps up to greet him as they shake hands. "Hey Andrew, glad you could join us. Now I don't have to spend the night outnumbered."

"I wasn't sure if I was going to make it. This new case has us all tied in knots at the station. But I think we've done everything we can for the day. Plus, I didn't want to miss our first Independence Day celebration together," he says as he leans in to kiss me.

Initially, he refused to kiss me until the first case that brought us back together was solved. And yes, I said back together because he once kissed me in high school and then didn't speak to me again because his parents didn't want him associating with riff-raff like me.

I just didn't know it at the time. I spent 10 years assuming he thought I was a horrible kisser. A decade later, I came back to town bearing a grudge. And deservedly so! And yes, every time we kiss now, my stomach still does flip flops. He's just that good.

He's tall and ridiculously good looking. Maybe too good looking. Gladys fawns over him whenever he's in Marcall's, and even Damien and Tom insist on reminding me how sexy he is. It's absurd, really.

"Wow, it is our first 4th of July celebration together, isn't it? Time flies when you're having fun, I guess," I wink at him. Of course, I'm having fun. I'm crazy about him.

Drew grows somber, "Now for the things that aren't so fun. I should fill you in on what we've learned so far because I know if I don't tell you, you'll just go out on your own and try to gather the information that way. And I don't want you interfering again."

Miranda and I make exaggerated innocent faces at each other. "Who us?" I ask.

Drew groans. I know it frustrates him that I keep ending up in these situations, and then I feel compelled to solve them. But I maintain it's not my fault. The excitement just seems to find me.

"I don't want anyone else to hear us, though," he says, glancing around. "It's bad enough I'm telling you as it is."

I glance at Miranda questioningly, and she nods her head.

"But I've never done this for real," I protest.

"Go ahead, you can do it. Just like we practiced earlier."

Drew looks at us, confused, as I concentrate on forming an invisible barrier around us. No one can see the barrier, but we can shout as loud as we want inside it, and no one will hear us.

I explain this to Drew once I've formed the barrier, but he wonders how we can know for certain that no one will hear us. Miranda, happy to demonstrate, shouts, "Hey you!" so loudly at a guy walking by that she makes the rest of us jump. But that guy doesn't even flinch, and neither does anyone else.

"Well, now that I've gone deaf," Miles says, looking at her with dismay while sticking a finger in one of his ears, wiggling it around.

I laugh and shake my head. That's Miranda for you.

Drew doesn't waste any time. "First, the coroner estimates the time of death at some time between 11:00 and 11:30 AM. Given that you found her at almost noon, he was able to pinpoint the time to a narrow window."

I gulp. I can't believe I got there shortly after she had been killed. I feel horrible. What if we had been able to interrupt the killer beforehand? She might still be alive right now.

Drew looks as if he can read my mind, "Don't do that to yourself, Char. Believe me, it's a never-ending cycle that you don't want to put yourself in. You couldn't have known what was happening, and even if you had been there – who knows, we could have two dead bodies right now."

He presses on, "And second, the dagger we found in Darla's chest belongs to Cody Murphy, and the only fingerprints on it are his."

"Oh no," Miranda blanches.

"I don't understand." It's a horrible crime, obviously, but why has Miranda gone pale?

Miranda explains, "Cody Murphy is a bladesmith, and he owns the metal works shop called Cody's Chromeworks. He's also a skilled knife thrower who puts on shows at festivals throughout the summer."

"Oh. Okay," I'm still confused by Miranda's reaction.

"Cody is Damien's cousin!" Miranda says.

"Oh," I respond quietly, shaking my head. "No wonder he told me everything is chaotic. This makes things way worse than they already were. Do you think he could have killed her? Cody, I mean?" Gladys' gossip about Darla being involved with her boss Harold plays out in my memory, and I have a sick feeling in my stomach.

"It won't do any good to speculate until we have more facts about the crime, and those won't come until tomorrow," Drew warns. "My advice is to just enjoy ourselves tonight and tomorrow when we know more, then we can help."

I agree reluctantly. Drew works so hard we rarely get an evening to enjoy like this, and I want to relish every moment. I also want to watch Miranda's firework display win first prize. Although if it doesn't win, I'm not sure I want to be around her. She'll be livid. Especially if she gets beat by this Penelope character.

Still, despite my better judgment, I'm itching to get in the middle of all of this. I know, I know, every time I get in trouble with these things, I swear them off, but I can't help it. And now, if Damien's cousin is in trouble, I want to help any way I can.

This one really is different. It's not just some random crime. It's tied to Damien's family. And since I moved back to Crested Peaks, Damien himself feels like family to me. So that makes this extra personal.

As I ponder all of this, I catch Drew staring at me. "You are staying put at least for this evening. I'd warn you to stay out of the investigation completely, but I know you'll just ignore me. But at least for now, I'm telling you to stay here."

"I don't want to be anywhere else, Detective McHotty," I tell him hoping to distract him by calling him the name that Miranda and Damien first coined. He purses his lips together and scowls at me.

"Nice try. Why don't you magic some slices in this bread?" he says, handing me the freshly baked loaf.

The four of us enjoy a decadent dinner full of bread, cheese, fruit, hummus, and wine. I love summer when fresh fruit bursts with color and flavor. Blackberries, raspberries, strawberries, and cherries are all at their peak and so delicious. I feel like I could eat the entire thing myself.

Miles picked up some fantastic cupcakes at Chloe's Cupcakes, owned by our high school friend and fellow witch, who recently left her job as a mortuary beautician – yes, it turns out there is such a thing - and opened a cupcake truck.

Miles brought some delightful red velvet cupcakes swirled with red, white, and blue frosting, topped with enchanted glittering gold stars that wink at us just like real stars. Aside from poor Darla and everything Damien's family must be going through, this has been one of the best evenings ever.

When the announcer's voice booms across the area, "Ladies and Gentlemen, please prepare yourselves for our evening's spectacular firework show starting shortly!" Miranda and I look at each other and squeal.

Then she reaches out to me and squeezes my hand. I'm so excited for her and nervous for me. I hope my display doesn't look too amateurish. I know it's just my first one, but it would be nice if people enjoyed it.

"If the judges will please take their seats, we'll get started."

Five judges gather to sit at a table on the podium. Three Supernaturals and two Non Supernaturals. As a judge, you can't enter the competition, nor can any of your family members.

Yes, Crested Peaks takes its fireworks competition seriously. The winner receives a whopping $500 in gift certificates to many of the area shops; which includes two ski passes good for any day during the winter. Did I already mention we take this seriously?

Marcall's Cafe donated a $25 gift certificate. That easily covers breakfast for two with coffee and a sweet to go. The show starts off with a display done by a witch who works at the pet grooming salon. It features numerous dogs and cats running and jumping about. It's really cute, and the audience clearly appreciates it.

The displays are mainly fireworks with stars and glitter and light, but the extra creative types add in features like laser lights and glowing streaks. The detail in some of the displays is extraordinary, and I have no idea how they do it.

My display goes third, and because I moved back here from New York City, I thought it would be fun to highlight the NYC skyline along with famous attractions like the Statue of Liberty, a Broadway show, and the Empire State Building.

Miranda helped me create the Statute of Liberty, bowing at the end. People applaud loudly, and Drew even grabs me and hugs me in the middle of it all; he's so impressed. I'm pretty impressed, too, actually.

Miranda is second to last. Her display is the actual shootout between Sheriff Thompson and a bank robber at the Hotel Glacier. Harvey was working as a bellhop at the time and was killed in the crossfire.

It was Harvey's idea, and the two of them worked on it together for nearly a year. The bullets seem to whiz over our heads and are so lifelike some of us duck in our seats. No wonder her shows are the stuff of legends.

Everyone leaps to their feet at the end, shouting and whistling. The thunderous applause goes on forever. Harvey stands on the uppermost balcony of the hotel and just beams as he bows and waves to his fans below.

I've never seen him so happy. Sometimes he gets grumpy when he feels left out in Crested Peaks. He has complained when he thinks we're only seeking him out for information about what's happening in the hotel. Can we help it if the hotel is frequently the hub of mysterious occurrences in town? But tonight, none of that matters, and he's all smiles.

Everyone crowds around Miranda, patting her on the back and shaking her hand. Several say it's her best one yet. I'm so proud of her and know that I'm lucky that someone with her talent is my mentor and my best friend.

Then she wins first prize with a 4 to 1 vote. When she vows to figure out which judge voted against her, Miles reminds her to take her win graciously. She can be a little competitive at times.

Drew drives the boys and me home. The rabbits chatter non-stop about everything they did that evening, and they tell me Stumpy even liked my fireworks display. After Drew drops us off, I remember what's happening in Damien's family, and I'm glad the café is closed tomorrow.

We originally planned to spend the day doing inventory, but now I think it will be just me. At least that means I get to sleep in. Now, if I can only convince the rabbits to sleep in. Stumpy is easy. I have to drag him out of bed to go to work as it is.

I'll text Damien in the morning to let him know he should stay home and be with his family. I'll see what we have on hand in the restaurant and take something over to them.

We were also going to work on the new donut recipe. So far, it's top-secret, but it will be a little bit Damien, and a little bit me. But it can wait too. Whatever his family needs comes first right now.

Chapter 5

The rabbits let me sleep until all of 7 AM, which, when you own a breakfast café, is still considered sleeping in. I text Damien and tell him that he should take as much time off as he needs. I know first-hand what it's like to be accused of a crime and how stressful it is.

When I arrive at the café though, Damien is already there. He insists he needs the distraction. "I have to tell you something, but you can't tell Drew."

"Is it about the case?" I ask.

"Yes. Maybe. I don't know."

I cringe. Damien himself has warned me repeatedly not to get involved in police matters. He thinks it's too dangerous, and now he's the one asking me to keep a secret. I remind him, "You know how mad Drew gets when I keep things from him. The best I can do is promise to keep it to myself only for the time being."

"If that's the best you can do," he pauses like he still isn't sure he should confide in me. "I saw Cody and Darla arguing the morning that she was killed. But I guarantee there's no way he'd kill anyone, ever!"

"You saw them arguing?"

"Yes, I noticed them from across the street, in front of Cody's shop, but I don't think they saw me. I couldn't hear them. It was just obvious they were in a heated conversation."

"Did anyone else witness this?"

"Yeah, I saw several people walk by and look at them as if they were curious about what they were fighting about."

"So, any of them might let the police know what they saw, or maybe heard, and know what the argument was about?"

"I suppose," Damien says thoughtfully.

"You're sure you don't know what they were arguing about?"

"Not a clue. I swear."

"I think we're safe keeping it to ourselves for now. But if it looks like it's relevant, one of us has to bring it up with Drew."

"Deal," Damien concedes.

"I have to tell you that yesterday, Gladys mentioned that she heard Harold the magician and Darla were romantically involved."

Damien looks defeated as he pinches the bridge of his nose. "If that's true, this looks extra bad for Cody, doesn't it?"

I gently rest my hand on his arm. "Keep in mind, just because Gladys heard something doesn't make it true. She is wrong on occasion."

"I suppose. Hey, by the way, is Harold an actual wizard or--" Damien starts.

"Nah. His magic is all sleight of hand," I assure him. "It's still a skill, of course, but it's all manufactured. They don't like to see real witches and wizards perform like that. The Supernatural Council feels it cheapens their gifts."

"I could see that."

"I sense that Harold is deceiving us, though."

"What do you mean sensed?" he asks.

"Miranda thinks I may have some kind of limited psychic ability."

"Whoa!" Damien's eyes widen. "That would be amazing! But how does it work?"

"I'm not sure myself. It's just that I seem to know things. But not all the time or anything like that. So far, it seems like it's only under highly stressful or emotional situations. And it looks like it's just now surfacing as I get better with my magic. When I watched Harold react to seeing Darla's body, I immediately knew he had some kind of secret he's keeping from everyone else."

"Do you think he killed her? Is that what you were sensing?"

"It's certainly possible. I don't know for sure what the deception is. What I do know is that when it comes to Darla, he's being dishonest."

"I know Harold and Cody don't like each other," Damien reveals.

"Maybe because they were both involved with her? And they were jealous of each other?"

Damien shrugs his shoulders. "I honestly don't think so. But would I bet my life on it? No."

"Last night, Drew said they questioned Cody at the scene, and he has a weak alibi, so they haven't arrested him, but he's been ordered not to leave town."

"Yeah, my aunt said he's at home alone, and not only grieving Darla but worried that he'll go to jail for a murder he didn't commit."

I nod my head. "I certainly know what that's like. It's scary and lonely."

"Do you mind if I go visit him? I know we're supposed to be doing inventory and working on the new donuts today since the café closed, but now I think I should stop at his apartment and offer my support."

"Of course, I don't mind! Go. Hey, maybe I should come with you? I can empathize with him, after all. Tell him to hang in there."

Damien looks at me suspiciously. "I don't have to be a psychic to know that you have an ulterior motive for that. As kind and generous as I know you are, part of me thinks you not only want to offer your support, but you also want to question him about the murder." Damien plants his hands on his hips and leans in close.

My cheeks turn pink. "Um, well, I don't think it would hurt after all. Just a few questions. Assuming he is innocent—"

"He is!"

"Then we need to find out who really killed Darla and make sure the true murderer is the one who ends up in jail, and not your cousin! Besides, if you get to blow off inventory, then I do too," I state emphatically. Maybe a little too emphatically. Anything to get out of inventory.

"Isn't there some kind of spell you can perform to automatically do this, so we don't have to?"

"You'd think so, wouldn't you?" I scratch my head. "I should ask Miranda."

"All right, let's go see Cody."

Chapter 6

We drive over to Cody's apartment, and when he answers the door, he looks like he hasn't slept in days, and his eyes are puffy from crying.

"Hey, cuz," Damien says grimly while giving him a bear hug.

"Thanks for coming over. It's still so hard to believe she's gone. And especially in that way," Cody swallows heavily as if he's trying to push down the thought of his girlfriend being stabbed and then left in the park.

"Cody, this is my boss, Charlotte."

"Hi Cody, you have my deepest sympathies."

"Oh, yeah, thank you," he sniffles. "Damien always talks about how great you are."

I blush. "Oh, my goodness, I don't know what I'd do without Damien."

"We just wanted to check on you and see how you were holding up," Damien interrupts.

"They tell me they found one of my daggers in Darla's chest. Mine! And that my fingerprints are all over it. Can you believe that? They think I killed Darla! I would never, ever, even think about such a thing! What am I going to do, Damien?"

"The police mentioned that you have an alibi for the time of the murder?" I probe.

"Yeah, I was at the hardware store buying a garbage disposal. The police are asking for a receipt, but for some reason, I can't find it." He then points at the box sitting on the counter.

"Then I came home and spent the morning installing it because my show wasn't scheduled until the afternoon. The next thing I know, the cops are banging on my door telling me Darla is dead and they want to talk to me about it. I never even got to say goodbye."

At this point, he can't hold back any longer, drops his head into his hands, and sobs loudly. I'm hoping to get some kind of reading from him too, but all I feel is pity and compassion for him. I can't read him. And I can't tell if he's lying about anything.

"Do you have any idea who could have done this, Cody? Did Darla have enemies?" Damien asks.

He sniffles again, "I know the girl she replaced was furious."

"Why did Harold hire Darla in the first place? Did the other girl quit?"

"No, she didn't. Harold fired her without an explanation and then immediately hired Darla."

Damien and I exchange glances. That can't be good.

Damien takes a deep breath like he knows what he's about to say is touchy, "Cody, I have to ask you this. Do you think something was going on between Darla and Harold?"

"She swore there wasn't."

"Did you believe her?" Damien presses.

"Most of the time, I did. Honestly, I hated that guy. He was always getting into her business, telling her how she could do better than me and trying to give her a bunch of advice. He even tried to talk her into going to community college. What business was it of his?"

"When he said that she could do better than you, is it possible he meant him?" I prod.

"I suppose," Cody responds with a shrug. "He may have wanted something, but I'm certain she didn't."

"Who is the previous assistant? Do you know her name?" Damien asks.

"Her name is Phoebe Reyes, and I think she's working at the Kwik Kopies Copy Shop now."

When the doorbell rings, Cody slides his hand down his face and groans. "If that's the cops again or another reporter, I can't take it."

"I'll handle it," Damien says as he moves toward the door. "It's your mom," he declares with a sigh of relief after peering into the peephole.

"Oh, thank goodness!" Cody sighs.

Damien opens the door for his aunt while taking the casserole dish from her hands. "I made you a lasagna, dear," she explains while Damien puts it in the refrigerator.

"Thanks, mom. This is Charlotte, Damien's boss," he explains when his mother looks surprised to see a stranger in her son's living room.

"Yes, of course, you took over your grandmother's café after she passed. How lovely to meet you, dear. Damien speaks so highly of you," she says, crossing the room to shake my hand.

"I promise you, Marcall's probably wouldn't even exist right now if it weren't for your nephew. He's a genius in the kitchen."

"Did he tell you it all started with the EZ Bake Oven he got when he was three years old?"

When I glance over at Damien, it's hard not to laugh at the horrified look on his face. "Why no, he didn't, and you must tell me more."

"No! That's quite enough already, Aunt Iris. Charlotte doesn't need to hear stories about me as a toddler."

"Well, why not, darling? She seems quite eager to hear them. Did he tell you that when he was only two years old, he told his mother that he wanted Micky Mouse underwear, and she said if he wanted big boy underwear, he had to use the big boy potty, so he did. Just like that!" Aunt Iris snaps her fingers for emphasis.

"Aunt Iris, please!" Damien shouts, while it takes every ounce of strength I have to keep from falling to the floor with laughter. I'm sorry that it's at Damien's expense, but it's a much-needed moment of levity. Besides, now I can use these stories later to really torment my talented chef.

"All right, fine, I'll stop with the stories. I do appreciate you stopping by to support Cody, though. He really needs his family right now."

"You should know, mom that people are saying that Harold and Darla had a thing," Cody tells her.

Iris screws up her face in disgust. "That man! I always suspected something was going on between him and those pretty young assistants that he hires." When she sees the look on Cody's face, she puts her perfectly manicured hand over her mouth. "Oh, I'm so sorry, dear. You don't really think something was going on between Harold and Darla, do you?"

"Like I told Charlotte and Damien, she always swore there wasn't."

"But you didn't believe her?" Iris asks.

"I don't know what to think right now, mom!" Cody says, throwing his hands in the air. "This is all just so messed up. My girlfriend is dead, and someone killed her with my dagger. Everything is just a huge mess."

Damien steps forward. "Unless you need us to stay longer, Charlotte and I should get going. We have a lot of work to do at the café."

"Nah, not at all, man, I really appreciate you coming," Cody says as he shakes Damien's hand and pounds his back, as they do one of those bro hug things that always amuses me. Like it's acceptable to hug as long as we do it like this.

"Charlotte, it was wonderful to finally meet you," he tells me as he gives me a real hug.

"Goodbye, darlings!" Iris calls out to us. "Look me up anytime for more stories about Damien's childhood."

"I'd love to!" I exclaim as Damien practically drags me out of the apartment.

But as we step out the door, he pauses for a moment. "Hey, cuz," he says, turning back. "By any chance, did you see Darla yesterday before she was killed?"

We watch Cody take a breath, but instead of just saying yes or no, it's like he's thinking of what the correct answer should be.

I don't need psychic powers to know he's about to lie to us.

"Um, no, I didn't see her at all yesterday. Why?"

"No reason, I was just curious," Damien responds, glancing at me.

"Thanks again for coming by you two. It means a lot to me."

"Of course, and I mean it when I say if you need anything, just ask," I tell him.

"Thanks, guys," Cody chokes back tears again as he softly closes the door.

"Wow," Damien sighs. "That was rough. Did you get any read about whether or not he was telling the truth?"

"Nope. Nothing. But since you saw him with her yesterday morning, we at least know he's lying about that."

"Yeah, that bothers me. I still know there's no way he killed her, but why did he lie about seeing her?"

"And there's still the matter of his knife and fingerprints."

Damien sighs heavily. "I know. This could get bad for him, couldn't it?"

"Yes, it could, but we'll do everything we can to clear him, right?" I insist a little more confidently than I feel.

"Definitely!"

"I think we should talk to Phoebe at the copy shop."

"Oh, I was hoping you'd say that!" Damien exclaims.

Given that Damien is usually the one trying to talk me out of this type of thing, I can tell he's extra worried about his cousin. He's become such a dear friend to me, plus Marcall's wouldn't be the success it is without him. I'm more determined than ever to get to the bottom of this.

"Cody said she was upset about losing her job," I muse, "so that might give her motive. And it's not like it was a secret that he and Darla were dating, so she'd know where to get the dagger—"

"--so she could set him up to take the fall!" Damien claps his hands excitedly.

I don't have the heart to remind him that this is a long shot and that this still looks really bad for Cody, even if he does have an alibi.

"Let's go back to Marcall's and get a flier. That gives us a good excuse to visit the copy shop."

Chapter 7

When we arrive back at the cafe, Stumpy is chasing a grasshopper around the parking lot, and the rabbits are sound asleep in the supply closet.

The inventory remains incomplete, but we have more important matters to attend to. I grab a flier from the counter, and we head down Main Street. One of the benefits of living in such a small town is that most places are within walking distance.

The shops throughout town are still decked out in red, white, and blue decorations. Of course, some are bewitched to do all sorts of fun things, including miniature fireworks displays. Independence Day always brings in extra tourists, and this morning they're strolling along the sidewalks one last time before heading home.

As a ski area, it's far busier in the winter, but I think it's just as beautiful in the summer. Temperatures are cooler up here too, so when it's 95 degrees and sweltering closer to Denver, it's milder and in the 80's here.

As we walk into Kwik Kopies, an eager young man wearing enormous, plastic red, white, and blue sunglasses greets us at the door. When we ask for Phoebe, I'm relieved to learn that she's here today, and we hurry over to her at the counter.

"Hi Phoebe," I say, making a point to glance at her name tag, hoping it won't look like we sought her out on purpose. "Can I get 50 copies of this flyer?"

She wordlessly takes the flyer from me, glances at it, and then walks over to one of the large copy machines lining the wall. She feeds my flyer into the machine, punches a few buttons, and then watches as the machine sucks it in and begins to work its own kind of magic.

She returns, presses a few more buttons on the cash register, and finally looks up at us. "That will be $12.50."

Damien and I share a look. Chatty Kathy, she isn't. "Don't I know you from somewhere?" I ask.

She regards me icily. I notice she's about the same age as Darla. She has long, shiny blonde hair and big blue eyes. I think that perhaps Harold had a thing for young, pretty women.

Maybe he even took advantage of them by offering them a job and preying on their vulnerabilities. What if Darla realized this and threatened to expose him, so he killed her?

"I don't think we've ever met," she says.

"But I'm sure that I know you from somewhere," I persist. She stares back at us and is clearly annoyed.

"Wait, I know! I saw you in a magic show once. You're the magician's assistant!"

Anger flashes across her features. "I was the magician's assistant," she growls.

"What do you mean 'was,' what happened?"

"He fired me for no reason and hired some other girl. A girl with no experience. He probably just did it to get in her pants."

I purse my lips and shake my head in feigned anger, "Men!"

"You're tellin' me! And I was really good, you know!"

"You were!" I agree, nodding my head so vigorously even Damien feels the need to join in.

"I have big plans, and working as Harold's assistant was an important steppingstone!"

"Big plans?" Damien asks.

"Broadway!" she announces with a flourish. We nod our heads again in unison as if we totally get where she's going with this. "I was out there performing and building my portfolio. It was just a matter of time before I was discovered. Hollywood types come through here all the time, and I know one of them was going to see me and realize how talented I was!"

She was right about the Hollywood types. We often see famous people here on their way to ski at Aspen. Although I doubt many of them take the time to catch a local magic show.

"I have 1,200 followers on my Instagram account!" she exclaims so loudly several people in the copy shop turn to see what all the fuss is.

"That many?" I murmur.

"It's not fair!" she shouts, pounding the top of the stapler that sits next to the cash register, causing it to bounce off the counter and fall to the ground with a loud clatter. "And now I'm stuck here in this dead-end job making stupid copies all day!"

She kicks the stapler sending it sliding across the floor so fast Damien has to jump before it hits his feet. I quickly glance around for any sharp objects that might be within reach. I'm genuinely worried about what might happen if a pair of scissors or a letter opener were nearby.

Just when I think we've really done it, she suddenly stops and collects herself. "You want to know something funny?" she whispers.

"Uhhh, sure?" I whisper back.

"I have it on good authority; it may not even matter anymore!"

An uneasy silence settles between us. "And why is that?" I ask. I can feel my pulse tick up. What on earth is she about to tell me?

"Let's just say I know certain things," she responds with a smug look. "Hey, your copies are ready!" she announces brightly. Now I'm wondering if Harold fired her because she's not the most stable person in the world.

Do I think she could have stabbed Darla? Absolutely. And what does she think she knows that the rest of us don't? She hasn't even mentioned Darla's murder. Does she know she's dead? Did she kill her, thinking that would bring her old job back?

"Here you go! Hot off the presses," she smiles as I take the still warm copies into my hands.

"Oh, one more thing," I add. "Did you work here yesterday by any chance?"

"You bet, I worked until noon when my boss closed the store early, so everyone could go to the festival. Why?"

"No reason," I tell her. "Thanks for the copies," I say, holding them up while trying not to let the obvious disappointment show on my face. For some reason, I was sure she wouldn't have an alibi.

Once we're out on the sidewalk, Damien and I breathe a sigh of relief.

"Wow, that girl is a little unhinged," Damien points out.

"You think?"

"I think she could have killed Darla, don't you?"

"She is pretty scary. But she has an alibi."

"So she says." Damien reminds me. "All we have now is her word for it."

I can't help but think the same may go for Cody.

Then Damien chuckles softly.

"What?" I ask, wondering what's so funny.

"Bubbles has more than 1,200 Instagram followers!"

Chapter 8

Damien and I decide we should at least attempt to tackle the inventory chores again and head back to the café. In the middle of our counting, we're grateful when Miranda shows up with drinks from her coffee shop. Espresso for Damien and a glowing green Matcha Latte for me.

Damien quickly whips up a snack of tortilla chips and homemade salsa for us. "Are you sure you're not a wizard?" I ask him. "Or do you just keep chips and salsa on hand for emergencies?"

"It was actually something I put together yesterday to keep me busy, so I didn't have to keep thinking about how much trouble Cody is in."

"I don't care how you came about this," Miranda says, her mouth full of chips, "this is fabulous!"

"Don't ever offer me salsa from a jar," Damien warns. "It's homemade or nothing."

Damien's entire family emigrated from Cuba when he was just a small child. He's fiercely loyal to his family and is incredibly talented at creating fresh, distinctive dishes from scratch. So many of our customers are convinced that I must add a bit of magic to his cooking, it's that good, but it's really all Damien. There's more than one way to create magic, after all. It doesn't have to come from a Supernatural being.

As usual, we gather around the table in Marcall's dining area to fill Miranda in on what we've learned from Cody and Phoebe.

"It sounds like Phoebe has quite the temper, doesn't it? Do you think she could have snapped and killed Darla?" Miranda asks.

"Or maybe she only meant to threaten her, and things got out of hand," I offer.

"But if she was only looking to threaten her, then how does that explain the fact it was Cody's dagger and fingerprints? I mean if Cody didn't do it--"

"--he didn't!" Damien interjects.

Miranda holds her hand up. "I'm just trying to make a point here," she reminds him. "Assuming Cody didn't do it," she glances at Damien, and he nods his head in agreement, "the killer had to wear gloves. It doesn't sound like a fight that got out of hand," she adds.

"Good point," I sigh. And even if we're sure Cody didn't do it, we can't ignore the fact it was his murder weapon and his fingerprints." Damien looks stricken. "Because we know the police won't just overlook it."

"And I saw them arguing before she was killed," Damien admits softly.

"Are you kidding me? What were they arguing about?" Miranda asks.

"I don't know. And Cody doesn't know I saw them. They were across the street from me by his shop, and I saw what looked like a contentious conversation, so I stayed out of it."

"Did you tell Drew?" Miranda asks.

He shakes his head. "Not yet."

"That could be really bad, Damien."

"I know, I know," he insists. "I just know that there's no way he killed Darla. Argument or not!" He takes a final sip of espresso when his phone chimes indicating that he has a text, but his jaw drops as he reads it. He looks up at us, his face ashen. "It's my aunt. They just arrested Cody for murder."

Chapter 9

After I insist that Damien leave to be with his family, I decide I'm not in the mood to keep working on inventory after that. On my way home, Drew calls to let me know that he'll bring over dinner and update me on the case this evening.

After the rabbits eat their veggies, and Stumpy eats his canned chicken morsels - the best part being the gravy he told the rabbits - Drew shows up with spaghetti and marinara sauce. And this time he remembered the garlic bread and it smells out of this world.

Ever since the Italian restaurant next door closed, due to the unfortunate death of Tony, the owner, I've really missed pasta with fresh tomato sauce. I've been eager to try the new restaurant that just opened in town.

And then, after Rita, the landlord, accidentally leased the space next door to Marcall's to a mafia kingpin, she decided to take it slow finding a new tenant. I'm looking forward to the day she can find a legitimate tenant, but I too, would prefer she take her time and find just the right one. Given that the same mafia kingpin tried to kill me last spring and all.

When Drew starts with a deep breath, I know a speech is coming. "Let me preface this by saying, as usual, I should be telling you that I can't share the details of an active investigation. But I know you'll obviously just get all of this from Damien anyway.

Plus, I'm hoping that by sharing this now, it will keep you from poking around where you shouldn't be later. And yes, I'm well aware that I keep saying things like this to no avail."

I nod my head enthusiastically. "Exactly."

Drew looks skeptical, but he continues. "When we checked out Cody's alibi, it fell apart. He couldn't have been at the hardware store the morning Darla was killed because the hardware store was closed the entire day."

"That's why he couldn't produce a receipt, I suppose," I point out.

"Kind of. Hang on a second, how do you know that?"

"Uhhhhh..." Rats. Busted.

Drew sighs in resignation. He already knows the answer. "Mr. Gallegos, the owner of the hardware store, remembers Cody buying the garbage disposal on the 3rd, not the 4th, like he told us. And, given that he was already our primary suspect, with his fingerprints all over the murder weapon that also belonged to him, it was enough to arrest him."

"It seems like such an obvious mistake, though," I surmise.

"What do you mean?"

"Let's say he really did kill Darla. Why give such a lame alibi? He went to the hardware store and then came home to install a garbage disposal? Seems like a weak and poorly thought-out excuse for someone who had just murdered his girlfriend."

"But then why give it at all?" Drew asks. "He may have panicked when we put him on the spot and failed to come up with a better excuse. Criminals aren't generally that smart. You'd be amazed at some of the stories they make up. Fortunately for us, it makes them easier to catch that way."

"But when Damien and I talked to Cody earlier today, he just didn't seem like an 'ordinary criminal,'" I argue, using air quotes for emphasis.

"And despite my usual warning, you're already investigating," Drew says, giving me that look.

"Oh, uh, well, uh, to be fair, Damien was going to visit his cousin anyway to check up on him—"

"--and you ever so helpfully offered to tag along," Drew interrupts

"Pretty much."

"I'm shocked," Drew says, rolling his eyes. "Is there anyone else I'm going to find out the hard way that you talked to, or are you willing to just come clean right now?"

"I had every intention of telling you."

"What."

"Cody mentioned that Harold fired his assistant to hire Darla and that she was angry and resentful about it."

"Phoebe Reyes."

"Yes, Phoebe," I add, my cheeks flushing because I knew I'd get in trouble for this before I even admitted it.

"She was near the top of my list. But what did you find out?"

"What do you mean she was near the top?" I ask.

"We arrested our primary suspect today, remember?"

"But you'll keep investigating, won't you? What if it turns out Cody didn't kill Darla? You don't want the killer to go free." I protest.

"We'll continue to investigate as the situation warrants. We'll need to build a solid case against Cody for trial."

"Are you looking at Harold the magician and Hilda his girlfriend as potential suspects?"

"We are. Are you?" he responds with one of his patented steely eyes stares. His intense green eyes get me every time.

"Remember how I told you last spring, that when The Jackal had her gun pointed at both the FBI agent and me, that I experienced some kind of energy surge throughout my body. And I knew she was going to pull the trigger?"

"Of course, I remember that. I was terrified when I realized you were in danger. And that's why it bothers me so much that you insist on investigating these crimes, instead of leaving everything up to the police."

I ignore the part where he pretty much glosses over what I just tried to tell him and skips right to the part where my life was in danger. "Yes, well, I experienced the same energy yesterday when I watched Harold discover that Darla was dead. And I know that he's hiding something."

"We've questioned both Harold and his girlfriend extensively, and both of their alibies check out."

"I get it," I respond. The obvious disappointment showing in my voice.

"I don't want Damien's cousin to be a killer either. But I have a duty to make sure that the person who murdered Darla pays for the crime."

"I understand that. I want the killer to pay too. I'm just certain it isn't Cody."

"All right, I have an idea," Drew says.

"Go on," I tell him, hoping that he's about to tell me that I've done such a good job sleuthing that he's changed his mind, and I finally have his permission to help him.

"Why don't we set aside all the cop talk and eat dinner instead?"

"Fine," I grumble. "I guess it does smell really good, and I'm hungry."

"And," he adds, waving a leafy green stalk in the air, "I brought parsley for Marshall and Marcus."

"Woo hoo!" Marshall shouts from the couch where he had appeared to be sound asleep but was probably secretly listening in on our conversation.

"All right!" Marcus chimes in from the same spot as they both scurry to jump down and sprint over to us.

Drew holds a sprig of parsley out for each of them but of course they both grab for the same one. A tug of war ensues where they squabble over the same piece while Drew just looks confused.

"Just give it a minute," I tell him.

When Marcus finally wins out by yanking the parsley away from his brother, Marshall sees the other piece Drew is still patiently holding, grabs it from him and runs off.

Poor Drew is so confused by all the drama.

"The other guy's piece always tastes better," I explain.

"I guess it's a good thing I don't have a brother," he replies, shaking his head in disbelief.

We spend the rest of the evening enjoying our delicious dinner and each other's company. It's rare that we get this much time in one week to just enjoy ourselves. Combine a relatively new restaurant owner with a career-driven police detective, and time together is a precious commodity.

After dinner, we stream the latest Marvel movie. And yes, I realize it actually came out a while ago, but have I mentioned how busy we both are? We both have to cut the evening short, though, because as usual, I have to be up at o'dark thirty to open the restaurant, and Drew will be at his job bright and early as well.

I don't know if Damien will be at work tomorrow or not. As far as I'm concerned, he can take as much time as he needs to so he can be with his family, but that will mean double duty for me.

Chapter 10

When I arrive at the café the following day Damien is already there once again preparing for the day. "I meant it when I said you should take time off," I lecture him.

"I know you did, but right now, I'm mostly just in the way at home. My aunt is beside herself; my mom is freaking out, the lawyers have been hired, bail posted. It's all a big mess, and I don't know how to help any of them."

Damien looks like he's carrying the weight of the world on his shoulders. "The one place that I know I can help for sure is here," he explains. "I told them if they need anything, they can just call me. Honestly, I think they were rather relieved to have one less person there hovering about."

"I still don't think your cousin is guilty, and we're going to do what we can here to prove that."

Damien nods his head. "Have you talked to Drew yet? Is there anything you're able to tell me?"

"You probably know more than I do. He just said that they know Cody lied about going to the hardware store on the 4th and that he was there on the 3rd instead. Considering his fingerprints were already on the murder weapon, they felt that was enough to make an arrest."

"Did you tell him that I saw Cody and Darla arguing that morning?" he asks, almost as if he's afraid to hear the answer.

"Nope. I feel like that's yours to reveal and I'm still not convinced it means he murdered her. Lots of couples argue without killing each other. I think you should just wait on that for now."

Damien sighs with relief. "I appreciate it. I just don't want you getting in trouble with Drew for holding back."

I shake my head. "I think I'm pretty much always in trouble with Drew for holding back information on a case. I'm not sure that one more is going to tip the scales either way."

"You're a good friend Charlotte Duffin," he tells me as his eyes shimmer with unshed tears.

"Let's get your cousin's name cleared, find out who really killed Darla, and then you can cry all over the place, all right?"

"It's a deal," he says gratefully.

"Do you happen to know why he lied about when he was at the hardware store?"

He shakes his head. "No, I haven't been able to talk to him alone, and I don't want to freak out my aunt or my mom any further."

"Because I think that's kind of key to the whole thing, and Drew hasn't said if Cody told them why he lied either.

When a sudden rush of hungry customers pours into the café, we're forced to put the conversation on hold. Business in the café is brisk all morning, but it's during a much-needed lull when I realize we're completely out of paper napkins. What kind of restaurant runs out of napkins? One that doesn't keep up with its inventory, I tell myself.

"Hey Damien, I've let us run out of the paper napkins. Are you okay by yourself if I run to get some at the restaurant supply store?"

"Of course, and while you're at it, we're almost out of straws too."

I sigh. "Maybe I should find a magical way to keep up with inventory."

"Orrrrrr," he starts with a glint in his eye, and I know what's coming next. "Maybe you should hire additional help. Even an assistant would help us both out. You know we have the customer base to justify it now."

He's right. And he's been on me for a while to hire someone. I'm really not being cheap. We definitely have enough income now to hire a person to help us out. It's just that Damien and I work together so well that I'm nervous a new person could throw off what seems to be our perfect rhythm.

And yet, if I don't get additional help, it may become too much of a strain on both of us. "Fine," I give in. "I'll start looking, but you have to be a part of the decision."

"Happy to assist you."

"But since I can't conjure up napkins and straws out of thin air, I better run down to the store before it gets busy again."

"Take your time. I've got it covered," Damien assures me.

Chapter 11

As soon as I get back to Marcall's from the supply run, Damien has a message for me. "Hey boss, Beatrice, the florist, dropped off a handful of pansies for the rabbits and says she wants to talk to you."

I look down at Marshall and Marcus, who are eagerly awaiting their treats. Marcus gets a yellow pansy and Marshall a purple one.

"Does Beatrice wanting to talk to me have anything to do with the two of you hassling her for treats?"

"I don't think so," says Marshall through a mouthful of pansy.

"We've discussed this before – about how you two keep pestering every shopkeeper on Main Street for treats."

"We don't pester them; we just give them sad eyes like this..." Marcus demonstrates his best pathetic look. "And then they give us stuff. It's awesome."

Marshall nods his head in agreement. Then he shows off his best sad face hoping for another pansy.

"You two are incorrigible," I scold while shaking my head and tossing them another pansy.

"Stumpy does it too," Marcus points out.

"And I've had the same discussion with him."

"How's that working for you?" Marcus asks sarcastically.

Great. I always wanted a rabbit with a smart mouth.

"I should get this over with now while I have the time. Hold down the fort again while I'm gone."

"Sure thing!" Damien responds.

I waggle my finger at the rabbits, "I better not be in trouble because of you." The two of them roll their eyes at me and scamper into the back. It's hard to get too mad at them, considering they saved my life recently. But they sure get around.

Fortunately, the Roses Are Red Flower Shop is only a few doors down because it's a particularly warm summer day. When I duck into the air-conditioned shop, I breathe a sigh of relief the moment the cool air surrounds me. I see Beatrice at the counter, but she's already waiting on a man, so I just wave at her.

"Hey, Charlotte! I see you got my message! I'll be with you in just a bit."

"Take your time!" I tell her. So far, so good. She doesn't seem to be angry with me. When she disappears into the back, the man at the counter turns around, and I gasp in surprise when I see it's Harold, the magician.

Even though I hear Drew's voice warning me to stay out of this, I determine that it couldn't hurt just to pay my respects. "Hi Harold, I was really sorry to hear about your assistant."

He looks pale and tired, and I study his face closely. Once again, I'm struck with such an overwhelming energy of knowing he's hiding something. It's so strong I put my hand on the counter for support. I really want to know what he's hiding.

"Yes, thank you," he mumbles with a distracted glaze in his eyes. I feel bad for pressing him, but I must get to the truth.

"It's a really horrible thing – what happened to Darla. Have the police told you anything?"

"Thankfully, they arrested her boyfriend Cody yesterday, which doesn't surprise me in the least. I told her over and over that he wasn't good enough for her and that she deserved far better than him."

Someone like you, I think to myself. "You obviously really cared for her," I point out.

"I did. I thought the world of Darla, and I wanted only good things for her." Tears swim in his eyes. "I'm ordering some flowers for her funeral right now."

"When is the service?" I ask gently.

"This Friday at 10 AM at the Mountain Chapel."

"That's a nice place. Very peaceful."

"Yes, I suppose it is."

"Were you there when it happened?" I ask.

"When what happened? When that good for nothing boyfriend of hers stabbed my Darla with his own dagger?"

"Um, yes?"

"Of course, I wasn't there. If I'd been there, I would have wrung his scrawny neck with my bare hands before I let him harm even a hair on Darla's sweet head."

These two had to have been having an affair. At the very least, that's what he wanted. Sure, that doesn't automatically mean that he killed her. But it makes him a serious suspect. Even if the CPPD thinks otherwise.

"Where were you when she was killed? I would think you would have been together getting ready for that day's show."

"We were scheduled to rehearse in the morning, but she never showed. I didn't think much of it at first. I thought that maybe she accidentally overslept, so I went through some of our routine myself.

"But when it got later and later, I got worried. She wasn't answering her phone, so I decided to look for her. And that's when I saw the crowd gathered, and there she was, on the ground." He chokes back a sob.

So, he doesn't have a witness for his alibi, and I know that he's lying about something. I have to assume at this point it's about her death. "You only hired her recently, right? To replace Phoebe."

"Yes, that's right. Did you know Darla? Were you friends with her?"

I'm in so much trouble for this one. "Yes, we were friends."

"That's so nice to know. I always enjoy meeting one of Darla's friends."

I'm already in this deep. I may as well keep going. "The one thing that I know she was most surprised about was when you hired her in the first place, given her lack of experience and all that."

Now he's looking at me like he's not quite buying the excuse that I'm nothing more than a friend of Darla's.

"Really? She never mentioned that to me. She said that to you?"

"Um. Yes. Don't get me wrong, she was thrilled to have the job. Just a little surprised, that's all."

"Huh." He studies me closely, and for a moment, I'm worried he'll recognize me as the one who found Darla's body in the first place. "And what did you say your name was again?"

I seriously consider giving him a fake name when Beatrice comes out from the back room.

"Harold, you're all set. Your incredible floral arrangement will be delivered to the church Friday morning. And we appreciate you trusting us with such an elaborate display for your loved one."

"That's wonderful. Thank you so much for your help. And it was nice chatting with you, young lady. Will I see you at the funeral?"

"Yes, of course," I tell him. Grateful that in his fog of grief, he seems to have forgotten I was making him suspicious. Yet my sense about his deception is stronger than ever.

"Charlotte, I'm so glad you could stop by," Beatrice coos. "I've been meaning to come over to the café forever, and I'm sorry I didn't get there sooner. Your grandmother was a wonderful woman, and I know she'd be pleased to see it doing so well."

I smile back at her. "I like to think so. Hey, I apologize if the rabbits have been bothering you for snacks. I can tell them to stop."

She laughs warmly as her kind eyes crinkle at the corners. She has deep brown skin and wears her braids piled high on the top of her head. I instantly picture her and my grandma as friends. "Nonsense, they aren't a problem at all. They're adorable the way they come around here looking for pansies and apple tree branches. I love their wiggly noses and that funny little cat who follows them."

"Oh, yes, they invited him to live with us."

She chuckles as if I'm just being silly. If only she knew! "It's amazing how well the cat gets around on his stumps. And how did he get that way, to begin with?"

"He says it's an old war injury."

Beatrice giggles. "You're so funny. You must get that from your grandmother."

I smile. "Gran was one of the funniest people I've ever known, and I never tire of hearing the locals share stories about her." I pause, hoping this seems like a natural segue. "Before I forget, can I ask about the floral display that Harold ordered?"

"Oh my, it's a sophisticated floral arrangement. One of the biggest I've ever done." She leans in and whispers. "And it was very expensive!

Anyway, your grandmother and I had discussed something before she died, but we never got around to implementing it, and I thought I'd see if you were interested. I'll give you a floral arrangement every week to display in the café, along with my business cards, so if your customers like it, they'll know where to go to get flowers."

"I love the idea of having fresh flowers in Marcall's!" I exclaim.

"Fabulous! Would you like an arrangement to take back now?"

"Sure!"

"I'll get one from the back."

She scurries to the back once again, leaving me to ponder my conversation with Harold. He's lying, and there's a good chance he killed her. Or maybe Hilda killed her, and he's covering for her? And he feels guilty. Better to pin the crime on Cody than him or his girlfriend. I don't know. It's all swirling together in my brain, and it's giving me a headache.

"Here you are, Charlotte. I hope you like it!" She hands me a beautiful arrangement full of pink and red gerbera daisies along with white roses. "And here are some raspberry leaves for those rascally rabbits!"

"You're too kind," I tell her. "Do you have something I could put your business cards in?"

"Of course. And here's some flower food to help keep them fresh. You should only need to change the water every couple of days. Thanks for doing this. I look forward to our partnership."

"Thank you for the flowers. They're beautiful!"

On my way back to Marcall's, I realize that I have to talk to Hilda as soon as possible. If Harold is hiding something, I bet she's involved. Especially if Harold was romantically involved with Darla in the first place.

Maybe Hilda's blackmailing him? Perhaps they were having an affair, Hilda found out and threatened to tell everyone. Harold killed Darla, and now Hilda is holding the entire thing over his head.

I'm so lost in thought that I barely realize that I'm back at my own café. When I walk in the door, Drew is there talking to Damien.

"Oh, hey there," he says, his face faltering a little when he sees the gorgeous bouquet in my hands. "Those are nice flowers," he points out, his smile somewhat forced.

I have to admit I'm a tiny bit satisfied that he looks jealous. "They are nice, aren't they?" I put my nose in them and inhale deeply while refusing to admit where I got them. I place them on the countertop with great care while concealing the business cards in my hand.

Damien looks back and forth between the two of us with an amused look on his face knowing full well where the flowers came from.

"I happened to be nearby and stopped in to say hello, but Damien said you were out," Drew explains, glancing at the flowers again. I know I should just come clean and put the poor guy out of his misery, but I can't help it. This is just too fun. If I have to watch half the ladies in town bat their eyes at him, then I get to have my own entertainment once in a while.

Gladys, who's old enough to be his grandmother, openly flirts with him every chance she gets. She's always commenting how she'd like to see him in uniform more often. Ugh. I try not to think about Gladys enjoying the sight of my boyfriend in his uniform.

"I'm glad I caught you before you left. You both might like to know that I just ran into Harold at the flower shop."

"Damien didn't tell me you were at the florist," Drew says, eyeing him suspiciously.

"Must have slipped my mind," Damien says while he's suddenly extra busy arranging a stack of napkins.

"Beatrice is giving us a fresh arrangement every week to display here. People like what they see and then visit her shop. We get pretty flowers in our café." I smile.

Drew looks relieved. "That's a good idea! But what about Harold? I'm sure you interrogated him," he says, giving me a stern look.

"We just had a conversation. I didn't realize he was going to be there," I point out.

"Go on," Drew says.

"He was ordering flowers, a very elaborate arrangement from the sounds of it, for Darla's funeral on Friday." Damien shifts uncomfortably. This must be so hard on his family. "He's still hiding something – I just don't know what."

"He killed Darla," Damien insists.

"I think that's a distinct possibility," I agree. "Or, what about his girlfriend, Hilda?"

"What motive does Hilda have for killing Darla?" Drew asks.

"Harold and Darla were romantically involved, Hilda found out, and killed her in a fit of rage."

Damien and I nod at each other. It seemed that simple to me.

"Do you know for a fact they were having an affair?" Drew asks.

"No, I'm just assuming that based on all the gossip I've been hearing."

"Uh huh. And did you ask Harold if he was involved with Darla?"

"Not directly, no, I just kind of hinted at it…" I trail off.

"As I've mentioned before, we've questioned Harold extensively about his relationship with Darla. Not only does he flat out deny any romantic involvement, so far, there's no solid evidence – only gossip – that they were having an affair."

"Maybe he wanted a romantic relationship, and she turned him down. Threatened to expose him." Damien suggests.

"That's always a possibility, and that's why we're still open to new evidence. We meaning the CPPD," he emphasizes.

"And once again, I didn't specifically seek out Harold. We just happened to be in the same place at the same time."

"And see that you keep it that way, or have you forgotten already that you were held at gunpoint by murderous thugs twice in the last year?"

"I haven't forgotten," I sigh.

"I don't want to worry constantly about what kind of trouble you may be in," Drew says as he gives me a quick kiss goodbye. "I have to get back to work now. I'll call you later. And how about dinner tonight at the Hotel Glacier?"

"What? That makes three nights in a row! I feel special."

"You are special," he tells me as I blush.

"See you later, Damien!"

"Bye, Drew!" Damien waves as Drew disappears out the door.

"Just so you know, I don't want what's happening with my family to affect you and Drew or even Drew and myself," Damien assures me.

"Your cousin is not going to prison for a crime he didn't commit, not if I have anything to say about it," I respond. "But I appreciate you wanting to keep things separate. I know it can't be easy."

"And Drew is right. You shouldn't put yourself in danger. Not even for one of my family members. I don't want to worry about you constantly either."

"I'm being perfectly safe this time, I swear." Damien looks at me like he doesn't quite believe me. The rest of the day, business is steady. I feel bad for Damien when we overhear several customers discussing Darla's murder. The news that Cody was arrested had spread quickly.

By the time we close, Damien and I are both ready to go home. He's eager to catch up with his family, and I want to get ready for my date with Drew. We rarely get to see each other this often in one week, and I intend to enjoy every moment.

I just wish there wasn't the issue of Cody's arrest hanging over us, but this is a good opportunity to push my argument that Cody didn't kill Darla.

Chapter 12

I turn my hair color deep emerald green for tonight's date. To match Drew's eyes, of course. There are daunting spells I can perform with witchcraft, which, if done incorrectly can have tragic consequences. Being able to change my hair color on a whim definitely isn't one of them. It's one of the best parts, and I love it.

But then I change my outfit three times, finally settling on a sleeve-less lavender sundress made entirely from lace with a v-neck front and asymmetrical hemline. I like it because it reminds me of something they'd wear in the 1950s, although without all the petticoats.

I pair it with bright yellow strappy sandals, and I'm finally ready to go. Just in time, too, because I'm applying a light pink lipstick when the doorbell rings.

"Drew's here!" the rabbits call out.

"Answer the door!" I shout back, laughing because I know they can't. I walk out into the living room to find the rabbits staring up at the doorknob as if they're trying to figure out a way to open it. It really is a good thing they can't do magic. They'd take over the town.

When I open the door to see Drew holding flowers, I have to bite my lip to keep from laughing. It's a colorful mixture of wildflowers. He sees me trying not to laugh and shrugs sheepishly. "Fine, I admit it, the thought of some unnamed admirer giving you flowers really bugged me. I realized I better step up my game."

Meanwhile, I see the rabbits eyeing the bouquet greedily. "You had dinner; these are mine!" I remind them.

"Oh," he says, holding the flowers up a bit higher as the rabbits give him their practiced sad eye look. "I forgot they like to eat flowers."

Drew follows me into the kitchen while I search for a vase. I easily pluck a vase from the uppermost shelf, and he laughs. I turn and look at him with a raised eyebrow because I don't understand what's making him laugh. "This kitchen isn't built for Damien, is it?"

"Ha! No, it isn't. But I won't tell him you said that." At 5 feet 10 inches tall, I'm not only taller than most women I come across, but quite a few of the men as well. I love that I actually get to look up at Drew, though. And poor Damien. I really tower over him. When I'm around his entire family, I feel like a giant for sure.

"We didn't really talk about the case when I saw him earlier at Marcall's. I'm not supposed to be discussing it with him, given that we have his cousin in custody for murder, and I didn't think he'd want to talk about it anyway. But how's he doing with all of this. How's he holding up?"

"He's doing the best he can right now," I explain as I try to arrange the wildflowers in the vase in an artful way. I'm no Beatrice, though, so I mostly stuff them in the best I can. "He insists that there's no way Cody could have killed Darla, and I'm inclined to agree with him."

"That's perfectly natural," Drew says, taking the vase from me and wandering into the living room with it. "Most families feel like that –

especially at first." He reverses course when he sees the rabbits eyeing him and places the vase on a higher shelf than he first planned.

When he does that, Marshall stomps his foot in disagreement. "But have you thought about what might happen if Cody is found guilty of murder? Will that cause problems between you and Damien? Since I'm on the police force?"

"I hadn't really thought that far ahead. Damien swears Cody couldn't have done this, and that's good enough for me. By the way, do you actually get family members who are instantly like, oh, yeah, he totally did it?"

Drew nods his head. "We do. That's always a little weird too. When they tell us 'we always knew this would happen someday.'"

As we head out the door, I call back to the boys, "Be good! Don't break anything, don't fight, and don't watch scary movies on tv that will keep you up all night."

"You sound like my mother," Drew points out.

"And how is your mother these days? She still consider me riffraff?" I ask.

He grimaces. "I haven't exactly mentioned the dating Charlotte Duffin part to her yet."

Drew and I had a thing for each other in high school. One day he kissed me, but when his friends and family found out about it they were furious that he was spending time with the orphan of criminals. He didn't speak to me again until I came back to Crested Peaks ten years later.

"Just do me a favor. When you do have that conversation, I don't want to be anywhere in the vicinity."

"I'm not looking forward to it myself," he says, opening the car door for me.

On the drive over to the hotel, I fill him in on my plans to hire additional help at the café.

"I think that's a great idea! The café is always so busy, and you and Damien put in a lot of hours there. Extra help might allow you to take some time off once in a while."

"You're one to talk. You work all the time!"

"If you and your familiars would quit stumbling across dead bodies, it would cut my workload in half. In fact, we had to hire a new guard to work in the lockup area, just to accommodate the bad guys your familiars catch."

"Oh sure, everybody is a comedian," I tell him, playfully, landing a punch on his arm. "Believe me, I'd be thrilled if they would stop finding crimes that need solving. But you didn't really hire a new guard, did you?"

He nods his head. "We did! We hired a new guard to service the lockup, but I guess it wasn't just for your bad guys. And I told him where he could get the very best breakfast burrito in all the land. And why don't you send the familiars straight to me next time they find a body? Given that I'm the true detective here."

"Even if they did track you down, you couldn't hear what they're saying. You need me for that," I remind him.

"We communicated pretty effectively when they let me know you were in trouble last time," he points out.

"I'll give you that one," I admit.

"Maybe I should get my own familiars."

"But you're not a wizard. A familiar in your case probably wouldn't talk to you."

"Oh c'mon, lots of people are convinced their pets know what they're saying," he points out.

"Oh, I understand that," I tell him, nodding my head. "And I don't doubt that their pet companion understands them. As a Supernatural, though, I'm able to interact with the familiars on an entirely different energy level that lets me understand them in return."

"How come you can't hear what Stumpy says then?"

"As much as I adore him, I'm not bonded to him the way I am the rabbits. And I think part of that is tied to Gran. When she passed, the connection that she had with them was somehow transferred to me."

"Did your grandma do that on purpose?"

"Knowing my grandma, I wouldn't be surprised."

Drew shakes his head.

"What is it? Why are you shaking your head?"

"Not in a million years did I picture myself falling in love with a witch."

Whoa. Did he just say, love? "You say that like it's a bad thing," I tell him.

"No! Not at all! This is all completely fascinating and exhilarating but still rather surprising. Considering we come from different worlds."

"Now that you mention it, who could have pictured me, the daughter of two con-artists, in love with a detective?" There, I said it too. The L-word. It's a night of firsts.

Drew turns and smiles at me as he pulls the car into a parking spot. He leans over and gives me one of his toe-curling, stomach flip flopping kisses.

We saunter toward the hotel, holding hands, and enjoying the summer evening. It cooled off somewhat after the brief rainstorm that surprised us earlier. The sidewalks are still damp, and the air smells especially fresh.

The sun peeks through the trees as it begins its daily descent behind the mountains. As we draw even closer to the hotel, we see Harvey out front executing his duties as the manager. As a ghost, he doesn't serve as the official manager, but he's actually quite useful to the hotel staff overall. Or a reluctant witch like me occasionally seeking answers.

"Detective Bailey! Charlotte! Hello!" he calls out.

"Hello Harvey!" we respond.

"Young love on a balmy summer's eve. I remember it well."

"We saw you enjoying your 4th of July fireworks display the other day."

"Wasn't that marvelous?" he shouts, clapping his luminescent hands together. "I couldn't have been more pleased. I take it you're here for dinner this evening?"

"We are," Drew responds.

"Everyone is talking about the arrest you made of that Cody Murphy fella."

Drew nods his head. "I'm sure they are. News travels fast in this town."

"I can't say I'm surprised about him," Harvey tells us.

"Why is that?" I ask, wondering if Harvey knows Cody or what he's heard on the down-low. Ghosts, similar to the animal familiars, tend to overhear a lot when people least expect it.

"They were here for dinner, just like the two of you, but on the 3rd. They were so dressed up, and I noticed young Mr. Cody seemed particularly nervous. I dare say that if he could have known how the evening was going to turn out, he would have been even more nervous."

"Why is that?" Drew asks.

"Because she rejected his very public proposal of marriage."

Drew and I turn to each other in shock.

"Are you sure?" I ask.

"Of course, I'm sure. He made a big to-do of it. The kitchen staff was asked to prepare an especially romantic meal and afterward place the ring in a glass of champagne. Our suitor got down on one knee. It was quite the production, with the entire restaurant looking on. We were all shocked when she said no. My heart broke for him. He was clearly humiliated. Although that's certainly no reason to kill her."

Given the shocked look on Drew's face, I'm guessing he had no clue either. "Has this come up in your investigation?" I ask.

"No, not at all. And I'm surprised we haven't heard about this before now. Especially the way this town gossips. Cody obviously didn't admit this. Does Damien know?"

I gulp. "No." My heart sinks as I realize how bad this looks for Cody. The worse this gets for him, the less festive I feel. If she turned down his proposal, that was probably what they were arguing about the next morning. The argument that we still haven't told Drew about.

Drew looks grim. "I'll need to check in with the station about this."

"I'm not really in the mood for a night out anymore anyway. This is really bad for Cody, isn't it?"

"I'm afraid it is," he admits.

"Harvey, I don't think we'll make it for dinner after all," I tell him sadly.

"Oh, that's too bad. I'm told the special tonight is delightful."

"Maybe next time," I tell him as I give him a weak wave, and we turn to leave.

"I can drop you off at home and then go into the station."

"Can I tell Damien about this?" I ask.

"I'd rather you didn't. Not until tomorrow anyway. I need to investigate this further, and I don't want it made public yet because the media will be all over it. 'Spurned lover stabs his girlfriend at town festival after she rejects his romantic proposal' isn't a headline I want to see just yet."

"I understand." I understand, all right. I understand that when Drew finds out Damien witnessed an argument between them, only mere hours after she declined his marriage proposal, he won't be happy with us for not telling him. I don't feel like it's my secret to tell, but I will let Damien know tomorrow that he should say something to Drew.

Sleep doesn't come easy for me, and when it finally does happen, I have disturbing dreams all night long. I wake up tired and grumpy and dread seeing Damien at work. I'm supposed to keep what we learned last night from him while I'm still keeping what he knows from Drew.

Oh, what a tangled web we weave, I mumble on the way into the café.

Chapter 13

Damien looks relieved to see me. "Charlotte! I'm so glad you're here. Did Drew share anything new with you about Cody last night at dinner?"

"Did Drew share anything new with me? No." At least that part really isn't a lie, I tell myself. "But I think it's time to tell him what you know about seeing Cody and Darla argue the day she was killed."

He takes a deep breath. "Yeah, you're right. It's already bad enough that Cody lied about which day he was at the hardware store. I don't want Drew to think that you especially are keeping secrets from him, and I never should have put you in that position in the first place."

"Say no more," I tell him waving my hand around to dismiss any guilt feelings he has regarding me. "Your family is important to you, and you want to protect them. I'm sure I would have done the same if I were in your shoes.

Thankfully, before he has the chance to ask too many more questions, the usual morning crush streams in, and it turns into an unusually busy day. The two of us are kept scrambling for hours trying to accommodate all the orders.

Then when all three of my furry little hooligans suddenly appear at my feet, I get nervous. "If you've found a dead body, I don't even want to know about it. I'm serious."

Of course, I say this out loud in front of several customers who all look up as if they're sure they didn't hear me correctly. And not only am I talking about finding a dead body, but I'm also openly conversing with two rabbits and a cat. It's a wonder anyone in this town ever takes me seriously.

"The lady in the coffee shop says you're to come right over," Marcus informs me.

"The lady in the coffee shop is Miranda, and you'll have to tell her that we're swamped right now, but I'll be over as soon as I get the chance."

Stumpy looks at me, confused. Right. I forgot. They can't talk back to Miranda; they can only relay her message to me. "If I give you a note, will you make sure it gets to her?"

Marshall and Marcus laugh. "If you give us a note, we'll just eat it," Marshall reminds me. Then he looks at Stumpy as if he's listening intensely. "Nah, because we'll just take it from you too and eat it."

"Never mind, I'm sure Miranda will understand. If it's that important, she can just come over here."

"She said if you tell us that you're too busy, we're supposed to tell you it's urgent and that you need to come right over no matter what," Marcus explains.

"Urgent? Is she okay? Is she hurt? Is someone robbing the store?" I try to peer over the heads of all the people in the café to see if I can spot something going on across the street. At least the shop isn't on fire or anything. I don't see people running from the store.

Then Stumpy winds himself in and out of my ankles, which is unusual for him. "He's telling you that you need to go across the street right now," Marcus presses.

If I don't go now, it looks like the three of them won't give up. "Damien, I'm sorry, but I have to run across the street for a moment."

"Now?" he says as he motions to the crowd in the café.

"I have it on good authority," I nod my head at the creatures still perched at my feet, "that it's urgent."

"Hurry back, would ya?"

"I'll pop my head in, tell her we're slammed, and come right back."

As soon as I head for the door, Marshall, Marcus, and Stumpy all go the opposite direction toward the back of the café. No doubt to settle down for one of their multiple daily naps in my office.

I jog across the street, fully intending to let Miranda know that whatever it is, it will just have to wait. When I walk in the door, however, my jaw drops. Miranda is at the counter talking to Hilda, Harold's girlfriend.

My first thought is to sprint over there, knocking people aside; I'm so excited. But then I remind myself to be cool. I stroll up to the counter as casually as I can possibly muster. "Hey there, Miranda." When Hilda turns to see who's talking, I say cheerfully, "Hello!"

"Hello," she responds. So far, so good.

"Oh, hey, Charlotte, do you know Hilda?"

"No, I don't believe we've ever met. I'm Charlotte, and I own Marcall's Breakfast Café across the street."

"Oh, yes, I've been hearing great things about that place, and I keep meaning to stop by. But things have been so hectic lately."

"Hilda is Harold's girlfriend," Miranda explains, keeping up the act.

"Oh, gosh, what a tragedy you've experienced recently. With the death of Harold's assistant and all," I start. Now I just need to figure out how to steer this conversation to get the right answers.

"I can't believe they found her in the park!" Miranda exclaims.

"And what a horrible way to go," I add. "Were you there when it happened?"

"When she was murdered? Heavens no! I was with Harold helping him rehearse for the day's show."

While I can tell Miranda notices the confused look on my face, Hilda doesn't seem to notice or care. Miranda crooks her eyebrow at me, but I shake my head ever so slightly so she knows not to question me further.

Harold told me that he was rehearsing alone and became concerned when Darla didn't show up. He never mentioned that he and Hilda were rehearsing together. Was it an oversight on his part, or is Hilda lying? "Do you and Harold rehearse the act together often?" I ask.

"Of course we do. I am his girlfriend after all. I'm an invaluable member of his team. Those young ladies he hires can be so unreliable." I notice the pinched look on her face when she utters the words, young ladies.

"The assistant who was murdered, she was new, right?"

"Yes, I'm not sure why Harold insisted on hiring her. I thought the other one was fine. She was a complete bubble head like all the rest, but even I was surprised when Harold fired her so abruptly."

"You don't think anything was anything going on between them, do you?" Miranda asks. It's bold, but it needs to be asked.

"I most certainly do not!" she practically shouts.

"I didn't mean to offend you, I've heard things, you know, about Harold and Darla, and the way I see it, we women have to stick together. I hate to see you taken advantage of. You seem like such a kind woman."

This seems to relax her a little. "I get it, I know that people talk and all, but I assure you, there was nothing untoward going on between my Harold and Darla. Harold is absolutely committed to me."

"I should be on my way now," she suddenly declares. "It was lovely to meet you, Charlotte. I'll stop by your café sometime."

"I look forward to it!" I tell her.

After she leaves, Miranda leans in close, "Well? Anything? Any kind of reading?"

"No, nothing. So far, Harold is the only one I can get a reading from."

"Do you think that means Harold killed Darla?" Miranda asks.

I shrug. "I still wish I knew. I think Hilda's lying about where she was the morning of the 4th, though."

"Really? Why?"

"I talked to Harold yesterday in the flower shop. He was ordering a huge flower arrangement for Darla's funeral, and he said that on the morning of the 4th, he was rehearsing for that day's show. But he was supposed to be rehearsing with Darla. When he realized she wasn't showing up, he went looking for her. That's when he saw the crowd gathered around her body."

"And you're still absolutely certain Harold is lying about something."

"Yes, no doubt. I still suspect that they may have been romantically involved. And maybe Darla threatened to expose Harold? Embarrass him in front of the entire town and get him in huge trouble with Hilda?"

"Which would be motive," Miranda points out. "But why Hilda?"

"Go back to the affair angle. Everyone in town is talking about it. What if she discovered Harold is sleeping with his new assistant? She's furious and murders her."

"More motive," Miranda says.

"Precisely," I add, nodding my head. "But that also gives Cody a similar motive."

"Jealousy!" we say simultaneously.

Chapter 14

By the time I remember that we were in the middle of a rush when I abandoned Damien to come over to the coffee shop, the café has completely cleared out. I must be the worst manager ever. The last thing the poor guy needs is additional stress. "I have to get back to Marcalls, but let me know if you hear anything new."

"But of course!" Miranda responds.

I hurry back across the street, fully prepared to grovel to Damien over leaving him without help, only to find him in the back humming to himself, hard at work on something.

"Hey boss, come try out my latest. I'm hoping you'll want to add it to the menu."

"What is it?" I ask. I think that we need to put the finishing touches on our new donut recipe, but now he must have something else in mind.

"Breakfast tacos!" he says, beaming at me.

"Please tell me it involves a waffle wrapped around a French toast stick!" I beg.

His face falls. "Er, no, not even close, but now I'm thinking it should have."

"Whatever it is, I'm sure it's great," I tell him.

"It's a soft corn tortilla, filled with pinto or black beans – customer's choice - cheese and eggs, folded over, and browned on the grill with just a hint of olive oil. Served with salsa, lettuce, fresh tomatoes, and sour cream."

"That sounds amazing!" I take a quick bite of one and swoon. They're so good. "The customers will love these."

Damien grins. "You sure you wouldn't rather have French toast stuffed in a waffle?"

"There's a reason you're the chef. Oh, you know what would be great with these?" I unashamedly talk with my mouth full because they're just that good. "That creamy cilantro sauce you were working on last month."

"You're right. I'll start on that again right away. It needed just a bit more tweaking."

I shake my head. "It was perfect when I tried it," I insist. Damien is a true artist when it comes to his cooking.

As I continue to enjoy this new breakfast taco, I'm pleasantly surprised to see Drew come into the café. "Hi, honey! You have to try these breakfast tacos Damien made." But then I see the look on his face and know that something is terribly wrong. "Hey, what's up?"

"This can't be good," Damien says, also noticing the look on Drew's face.

"I wanted to come tell you this in person. Cody confessed this morning."

"Confessed to what?" I ask, still sure that Cody did not kill Darla.

Drew looks at me like I'm daft. "To killing Darla," he says softly.

"How is that even possible?" Damien asks in shock. He drops into the nearest chair, his head buried in his hands.

"He says he doesn't actually remember doing it. But that he must have been drunk, killed her, and then went home and passed out."

"What? No way! He's been sober for three years!" Damien exclaims. "He wouldn't do that!"

"He claims that the morning of her murder, he and Darla argued about the proposal and Harold. Cody was frustrated that Harold was trying to influence Darla too much. We also tracked down several witnesses who heard them arguing in front of Cody's shop the morning she was killed."

"Proposal? What proposal?" Damien asks.

Drew's eyes dart over to mine while Damien looks completely lost. "We have discovered only recently that Cody proposed to Darla on the 3rd at the Hotel Glacier, but she said no."

"This is insane!" he shouts. "Did you know he proposed to her?" he barks at me when he notices I don't look surprised at the news.

"We just found out about that last night, and I insisted she keep it to herself," Drew explains.

"I would have told you right away if Drew hadn't sworn me to secrecy." I'm hoping Damien remembers I kept his secret too.

"Er, about the argument they had in front of Cody's shop," Damien begins as if he read my mind, and he and I look at each other guiltily.

"Why are you two looking at each other like that? Are you keeping something from me?" Drew asks.

I open my mouth to confess when Damien does it for me.

"I saw them arguing. I didn't actually hear them, but it was obvious they were fighting. I told Charlotte about it, but I too, swore her to secrecy. She insisted this morning that I tell you, and I agreed. I had planned to talk to you about it after we closed today..." he trails off, looking like he might cry. "I take full responsibility," he insists.

Drew glares at me. "We'll discuss that later," he grumbles. "But since you only saw them and didn't hear them and obviously can't tell me what they were arguing about, I'm inclined to let Damien slide for now."

I gulp. It seems like I'm always getting in trouble where these things are concerned.

"As I was saying," Drew continues, giving me a salty look. "Cody claims that even though he doesn't remember it, he bought a bottle of vodka, after he and Darla argued. Then he went home and drank it, staggered to the festival, stabbed Darla, returned home, and blacked out."

"We already know he was lying about going to the hardware store on the 4th, but he was so convincing when he said he spent the morning installing the garbage disposal," I argue. I feel sick to my stomach. I was sure, along with Damien, that he was innocent.

Wouldn't the police have noticed that he was hungover when they originally went to question him? Wouldn't they have smelled it on him too, if he'd had that much to drink? Did anyone note this, to begin with?

"How could someone blackout to that extent?" I ask. "That he would stab someone and not even remember it?"

Damien shakes his head. "When Cody was drinking, he said he would often blackout and then not realize how he ended up in certain places. A park bench, a stranger's house, a jail cell. He'd have no recollection of where he'd been or what he'd done."

I still can't wrap my head around any of this. "If he really stabbed her, wouldn't he have blood on his clothes when he got home?"

"Murderers often dispose of their clothes in a random trash dumpster once they realize they're soaked with the victim's blood," Drew explains.

"Well, are you looking for them?" I practically shriek.

"We are still investigating this," Drew insists.

"Was there an empty vodka bottle at his condo?" I was sure I had him there.

"We found several bottles in the dumpster behind his condo, and we're dusting them all for prints as we speak."

"You found bottles but no bloody clothing?" I press. "What about receipts for the liquor store?"

"Are you asking if I know how to do my job?" Drew asks.

"Of course not. I'm just thinking out loud here."

"My aunt must be wrecked," Damien says.

"Go to your family. I can cover for you," I insist.

"Yeah, I better do that," Damien replies as he wanders to the back in a daze to collect his things.

"Call me if you need anything!" I shout out as he leaves. "I mean it!"

What a tragic situation all around. A young woman stabbed to death, and one of my dearest friends has a family member who confesses to killing her in a drunken stupor. None of it makes any sense. And now that Damien has left, I'm alone with Drew. Uh oh.

"I don't really have time to lecture you right now, and I doubt it would do any good anyway, but you have to know that you can't withhold possible evidence from me ever. You have got to trust me enough to let me do my job, Char.

"If you two had told me this in the beginning, I could have asked Cody about it early on. Maybe he would have at least told us about the proposal and the argument. It would have looked better coming from him."

"I get it," I sigh. "Thanks for coming over here in person. I think that meant a lot to Damien."

"Of course. Happy to do it. I just wish I had better news for him. I have to get back to work now, but I'll call you later, all right?"

Yikes. He doesn't seem very happy. I hope I'm not in too much trouble.

Chapter 15

After I close the café for the day, I duck into Bean Around a Bit again for a quick pick me up. The shop isn't very busy at the moment, so Miranda takes a break too, and I update her on Cody's confession. "I saw on the internet that Cody confessed earlier. Are you shocked? You were so certain he didn't do it!"

"This is going to sound weird, but I still don't think he did."

"Really?" she asks.

"He's claiming that he drank himself into a stupor, went to the festival and killed her, then came home and blacked out, but doesn't remember doing any of it."

"Then why did he confess? This is very confusing. How could he kill someone and not remember it?"

"My thoughts exactly. Damien said that Cody has been sober for several years, but when he was drinking, he'd drink so much that he would blackout and not remember anything."

"What would drive him to drink after all these years, though?"

"That's where it gets complicated," I admit. "Last night, Drew, and I went to the Hotel Glacier for a dinner date, and Harvey told us he saw Cody propose to Darla there on the 3rd, but that she said no."

Miranda's jaw drops. "Oh, that's awful. And so maybe he drank himself senseless because he was so devastated? And then he just lost it and killed her? What if it was all about being jealous over Harold!"

"It looks like that's what he's confessing to."

"How's Damien holding up?"

"He left work early to be with his family."

Meanwhile, as we're discussing how horrible the situation is, I happen to notice the two guys at the next table are complaining bitterly about people they work with. I don't really pay close attention until I happen to hear the words Kwik Kopies. Then I really perk up when I hear one of them say something about, "...that dim whit Phoebe."

At first, I'm worried that I'm imagining things, given my obvious interest in Phoebe. But I motion to Miranda to be quiet anyway. She raises an eyebrow as I gesture to the table next to us. I consider using a volume-increasing spell on them, but they're already quite loud and getting louder.

"She gets away with everything!" the tall skinny one with glasses proclaims.

"Phoebeeeeee!" the redhead groans as he throws his hand against his forehead while waving the other one around in what I gather is supposed to be a dramatic gesture. "Has she mentioned she's going to be a Broadway star?"

Glasses laughs. "Only 437 times by my latest count."

"What did she do this time?" redhead asks.

"You know how slammed we were the morning of 4th of July since we were closing early?"

"Yeah."

"She took off right in the middle of her shift with no warning! She was acting extra weird all morning and then tells me she's leaving that she has somewhere she has to be and needs me to cover for her. I told her no way, but she left anyway. Then she comes back right before noon, and I notice she's in different clothes. And she was in this super happy mood."

I stare at Miranda, my eyes like dinner plates.

"What is it? What's wrong?" she asks. "Are you all right? Are you having a stroke?"

"No!" I hiss. "Didn't you hear what those two guys just said?"

"Uh. No. I wasn't really paying attention."

"Phoebe, the person they're complaining about, is Harold's former assistant!"

"Annnnnd?"

"Who he replaced with Darla!"

"Ohhhhh," she responds, comprehension dawning on her.

"When I asked Phoebe where she was the morning of the 4th, she claimed she was working, but her co-worker just said she took off and came back right before noon, which would give her plenty of time to kill Darla!"

"Oh, dear, that sounds really suspicious."

"And he just said she changed clothes before coming back!"

"You think she had Darla's blood on the other clothes?"

"Maybe! And that would explain why they haven't found any of Cody's clothing with Darla's blood on it. She also told me, after she ranted about how angry she was, that Darla had cost her a chance at stardom.

"And that she had it on good authority that she wasn't going to have to worry about losing that job anyway. What if she said that because she killed Darla and knew she may be getting her old job back?"

"It's crazy to think about, and yet..." Miranda starts.

"Any crazier than Damien's cousin blacking out drunk for the first time in three years and killing her with no memory of any of it?"

"That's a good point."

"And she has motive after all. You should have seen her at the copy shop. She was furious."

"What do we do next? Should we tell Drew?" Miranda asks.

"He'll just dismiss it and remind me that Cody already confessed," I insist.

"So, it's up to us to follow up on this lead?"

"Definitely! We have to talk to her!" I demand.

"Right now?"

"Every moment that we wait is another moment that Cody sits in prison for committing a crime I don't think he did."

"Let's go then!" Miranda agrees.

We jump up from our seats as she calls out to one of her clerks to look after the shop while she's gone. I tell her to bring one of her drink menus, so we have an excuse to get something printed. An excuse other than catching a murderer, I mean.

When we walk in the door of Kwik Kopies, I'm dismayed that there's no sign of Phoebe. I approach a young woman at the cash register. "Excuse me, is Phoebe working today?"

She snorts. "Phoebe? She flounced in here an hour ago and quit."

Gulp. "She quit?"

"Yep. No notice or anything. Said she had to leave town fast, that she was off to become a Broadway star, and the rest of us losers can suck it."

I look over at Miranda, my heart racing. This can't be good.

"She said she had to run home to pack and that she had a bus ticket for a 4:00 departure."

I glance at the clock on the wall.

"We have 15 minutes to get to the bus station!" Miranda yelps as we race out the door.

The problem is the bus station is at least 20 minutes away by car, under the best of circumstances. It's close to the main highway, and a lot of people ride the bus up from Denver to ski in the winter. It still runs in the summer but on a limited schedule.

We dash to Miranda's car because it's closest, and while she drives as fast as she can get away with, I know it still isn't enough. "Isn't there some sort of spell to make us go faster?" I ask.

She shakes her head. "There is, but it just isn't safe with all these other cars around."

"Rats! Why can't the whole witches on broomsticks thing be real?"

"If you knew how many times I wished for that! One of us has a boyfriend who is a detective, though."

"And?" I ask, not sure how Drew can help us get to the bus station faster than magic.

"And while we can't hold up a bus, not from this distance anyway, the CPPD could call the bus station and ask them to hold the bus, couldn't they?"

"If I ask Drew to do this, and we're wrong, I think you could have another homicide on your hands," I warn.

"Oh, nonsense. He wouldn't kill you. He may just stop speaking to you."

"Gee, thanks, that's a huge comfort."

"I'm just teasing. You may just have to do some serious groveling for a while, though."

"Miranda, if we're wrong about this..."

"If we're right, then an innocent man will rot in prison while the real killer gets away on a bus!"

I agree, reluctantly, "Fine. I'll give it my best shot." I pull out my phone to call Drew.

"Hey there, what's up?" he says as he answers.

"I need a huge favor from you."

"Anything, as long as it doesn't involve inappropriate police investigating," he responds.

"Uhhhhhh."

"Charlotte Duffin, what have you done?"

"I haven't done anything, really, I mean not yet, but I need you to stop a bus."

"A bus? Have you been watching Speed again? Please tell me you aren't driving an out-of-control bus with a bomb on board because let's face it, that's kind of something you'd get yourself into."

He's not wrong there.

"I need you to call the bus station and prevent one of their buses from leaving."

"On what grounds? That's a very serious request you know, it's a huge headache for the bus station, plus all of its passengers. Something like that can have far-reaching implications. Why do you want me to stop it?"

"We think Darla's killer may be on a bus trying to leave town." The long uncomfortable pause makes me sweat a little. Miranda points at the dashboard clock, indicating that it's mere minutes away from 4:00. I shrug my shoulders at her to show I don't know what more I can do.

"Darla's confessed killer is downstairs in lockup awaiting transfer to the County Jail. I just saw him." Drew sounds like he's trying to be patient but is struggling with it.

"It's just that I've been following a lead and—"

"Why are you still following leads?" he cuts me off. "Especially if it involves chasing down a bus. You're supposed to leave that up to the police."

I press on. "The girl who used to be Harold's assistant--"

"Phoebe." Drew breaks in.

"Yes, Phoebe."

"She has an alibi for the morning of the 4th," he insists.

"Well, yes, but how did you know? Earlier, you weren't sure you needed to question her." I remind him.

"After you insisted that she might be a worthy suspect, I decided you could be on to something."

"Really?"

I can hear him roll his eyes through the phone. "Don't get excited. I said I thought you might be on to something." He sounds gruff, but now I can hear him smiling. "She said she was at work that morning, and her timecard confirms it."

"That's what she told me too, but I just overheard two of her co-workers talking at Bean Around a Bit. They say she skipped out mid-morning and asked one of them to cover for her. He also said she came back a while later wearing different clothes.

"When I went back to Kwik Kopies just now, to see why she lied to me in the first place, they said she quit suddenly and was leaving town on the 4:00 bus today. I think she may be running away, assuming the coast is clear, now that Cody has confessed."

"You're giving me very little to go on here, Char. I need something far more than that to ask a bus station manager to hold up a bus, along with all its passengers, based on a long shot. And then what? Ask them to pull Phoebe from the bus and force her to wait until I get there? There just isn't enough substance here. I'm sorry."

"That's okay, I understand. It's just hitting 4:00 now anyway, so it may be too late as it is."

"I have to go now; my captain is urgently signaling that he needs to talk to me. Look, I know that you just want to help your friend's cous—"

"--I want the true killer to be punished – whoever that is." I remind him.

"And I get that. I really do. I appreciate that you have such a passion for justice. I'll call you as soon as I get off work, how about that?"

"All right, I'll talk to you later."

By now Miranda and I are almost at the bus station. But it's 4:05 and we're sure that the bus has too much of a head start anyway, when lo and behold, a bus pulls out of the station. We look at each other and squee with excitement.

"Wait. How do we know that's even the right bus?" I ask.

"Because the last bus leaves at 4:00. It has to be it! They must be running late."

"But now what? We can't follow it forever. We don't even know where it's going," I point out.

"It's much safer to stop it here before it gets on the highway."

"Safer? What are you planning to do?" I ask. I'm picturing Miranda forcing the huge bus off the road with her Volvo, and I'm wondering what I signed up for. But of course, Miranda meant by using magic.

I watch her concentrate hard on the bus as it gets slower and slower until the driver signals that he's pulling off to the shoulder, where the bus lurches to a stop. I can't believe she just stopped a bus.

We jump out of her car and jog up to the door. Except now I wonder what we're supposed to do next. "Leave it to me," Miranda says upon seeing my confusion. She knocks on the door, and when it swings open, she asks, "Having problems?"

The driver throws up his hands. "I don't know what happened. It just quit."

"I'll take a look at it for you. I'm a mechanic," Miranda offers.

I stare at her like she's really lost it this time, but she pushes me forward. "Find Phoebe," she whispers.

Of course. I climb the bus steps while the driver stares at me awkwardly. "She's really good. I'm sure she'll have it fixed in no time," I reassure him. I scan the passengers' faces, noticing a mixture of frustration and confusion. Relief washes over me when I see Phoebe sitting in the middle.

"Hey, Phoebe!" I call out as I wave to her. The other passengers turn to look at her while she gawks at me like she has no idea who I am. And suddenly, I'm not sure what to say. Hey, are you skipping town because someone else confessed to the murder you committed? And if she really did murder Darla, I'm now confronting a killer on a bus full of people.

This is looking like a very bad idea and may not have been the smartest move to make by ourselves. Maybe Drew is right. I need to stop putting myself in these situations. But I refuse to let Cody sit in prison for a crime he didn't commit. Even if he thinks he did.

I have to wing it the best I can, and if necessary, I hope I'll have the skills to use any witchcraft I might need. "We stopped by the copy store today to have some menus printed, but they said you quit."

Finally, she recognizes me. "I've been offered a part in the chorus for an off-Broadway production, so I'm going to New York."

"Oh, I see," I respond.

I don't know if that's even true, and it still doesn't explain her sudden departure from work on the 4th of July. "How did you get a part like that?" I ask.

"I guess it doesn't really matter anymore, now that I've quit, but I snuck out of work on the 4th of July and auditioned for a producer who happened to be in town. I was sure I'd get fired because that jerk wouldn't lie for me, but then he did, and everything worked out anyway."

Oh. Wow. This is embarrassing. "So, when you mentioned to me that you didn't think Harold firing you may not matter anymore—"

"--I was saying that hoping that I'd landed the part and would be leaving this stupid town," she interrupts. "Although I had no idea when I said that Darla had been murdered by her boyfriend! Wow, what a mess. Turns out maybe I could have got that job back!" she laughs but then stops when no one else laughs along with her.

I'm horrified when I realize the truth. Phoebe didn't kill Darla, and we've disabled an entire bus for no reason. And does this mean that Cody really did kill Darla? If Drew finds out we did this. I gulp.

"Congratulations, Phoebe!" I exclaim. "I'm sure you'll be great. I'm going to check on my friend and see if she needs any help; I'll be right back." I scamper from the bus as everyone stares at me, then I run around to the engine where Miranda pretends to be making the repairs.

"Hey, what's happening?" she asks. "Did Phoebe confess? Is Drew on his way over to lock her up?"

"We've screwed up big time! Just get the bus going now!" I whisper in a panic.

"Seriously? What happened?"

"Just do it! I'll explain everything later!"

"No problem," she declares as she holds her hands over the bus engine, and it roars to life. Inside the bus, the passengers cheer. If only they knew. Miranda slams the hood shut, and we pause briefly in front of the door.

"Thanks, ladies!" the driver shouts as he closes the door and prepares to drive away.

I practically drag Miranda back to the car as the passengers continue to cheer and wave at us. I'm mortified.

"What on earth happened back there?" she asks, still confused over our abrupt departure. "And why is your face all red?"

"Drive!" I urge. "We need to get away from here as quickly as possible before anyone finds out."

"Oh, wow, did you hex someone?" Miranda asks as she quickly drives back toward town.

"Hex? No! I found out why Phoebe lied about not being at work the whole time on the 4th of July and why she's leaving town, though." I proceed to tell Miranda about how the conversation went down. Her mouth drops open in a silent O.

"We chased down a bus and forced it to stop for no good reason?"

"Yep."

"After Drew told us it was a big no, no."

"Pretty much," I respond.

"Yikes. Do you think they'll tell on us?"

I cringe. "I hope not. I mean, they don't really have reason to, considering the bus driver thinks the bus just had some kind of malfunction that you repaired for him. I can only hope Drew never finds out about this."

"You and me both, sister."

I hate the thought of keeping anything from Drew, but I'm pretty sure I hate the thought of going to jail even more.

"Does that mean Cody really killed Darla?" Miranda asks.

"I suppose it could. It rules out one of our suspects," I point out.

We fall silent the remainder of the drive back to town. My heart is heavy now that I realize Phoebe didn't kill Darla. I got my hopes up too high when I convinced myself that she was a likely suspect.

Sure, that still leaves Harold and Hilda, but it also still leaves Cody. What if he really did blackout and kill her? Now I just feel sick to my stomach. Miranda drops me off at Marcall's while she goes to park her car. "I'm sorry things didn't work out today," she says.

"Me too," I respond sadly.

Chapter 16

I trudge back into Marcall's thinking about what a mess everything is. I'm glad I didn't mention anything to Damien before we went on our wild goose chase.

And what happens when Drew finds out that we used magic to stop a bus that we shouldn't have in the first place? I feel like I've made such a mess of things.

I'm only slightly cheered up when I remember that it's Wednesday which means the Crested Peaks Farmer's Market takes place this evening. "Who wants to go to the farmer's market?" I call out in the quiet café.

No sooner do I get the words out of my mouth when Marshall, Marcus, and Stumpy all tear out of the back room. "We want parsley!" Marshall demands.

"And beet greens!" Marcus adds.

"What about you, Stumpy? Do you want something from the farmer's market?" I ask.

"He wonders if they have mice there," Marshall answers for him.

"Eww, no, we're not looking for mice just for you."

Marshall looks at Stumpy again and then turns back to me. "Crickets?"

"Gross. No animals and no bugs. Not on purpose anyway. How about some freshly grown, organic catnip?"

"He says okay," Marcus offers. "But he wants to know if you'll pull us around in the wagon."

"I suppose." How do I get talked into these things? I get the wagon out, and the three of them pile in, Stumpy with an assist by me of course, and we head off to the farmer's market down the street.

At every stand we visit, that has some kind of vegetable or fruit or greens, the rabbits are full on sad face. As if they haven't eaten in days and are desperate for a fluffy carrot top or a fresh radish.

At this point, they won't need dinner when we get home; they'll have eaten their fill by the time we're done here. Even Stumpy gets excited when we spot the Five Dachshund Bakery, which has delicious crunchy cat treats in his favorite flavors like chicken and tuna.

Our final stop of the evening is the Thai One On Food Truck that Damien is always raving about, but I have yet to try. I order pad thai and spring rolls. I know, about as unimaginative as one can get, but I just love it. The noodles and the peanuts and the spicy and sweet mixture just push all the right culinary buttons for me.

"Hi, guys!" the young woman who waits on me greets my companions in the wagon. Suddenly they all sit up extra straight, waiting for the inevitable treat. She gives each of the rabbits a fresh cilantro sprig and for Stumpy a small bite of chicken.

"You obviously know these characters," I point out.

"Of course!" she chuckles. "They stop by all the time looking for treats."

"I hope they're not too much trouble. I know they hit up every shopkeeper in town. I'm just grateful no one has complained yet."

"How could anyone complain? They're the cutest things ever! And you must be Charlotte, by the way."

"I am, and you are?"

"I'm Aranya Bunmi, my parents own the food truck, and I just help out from time to time. I'm a culinary student at Colorado Mountain College. I know they secretly expect me to join the family business after I graduate, but I've been working in the family business since I was 9.

As much as I love food, I'd like to try something different. At least while I'm in school, you know. But anyway, I'm just blathering on. Damien and Tom are regulars, and they're always talking about how great you are."

"They are too kind. I'd be lost without Damien. In fact, business is so good I need to hire someone to help us."

"Seriously?" she asks. "Could I put in an application? I'd love to work with you and Damien. I'll do whatever. I just need experience in another restaurant. I need experience working for someone other than my parents."

"Oh," I hesitate. "I would take you in a heartbeat, but I don't want to take you away from your family's business. I know I'd be really upset if someone lured Damien away from Marcall's."

"I'll still be available to help out on the food truck. I promise you won't be taking me away at all. I just need to branch out."

"Well, these three seem to really like you," I tell her, nodding my head at the familiars who are still giving her their best sad eyes. "Can you come by tomorrow morning around 10, and we could talk more?"

"Of course, I can!" she cries as she gives a little hop and claps her hands together. If she's always this enthusiastic, then I may have a real catch here.

"Great! I'll see you tomorrow then," I tell her as I take the warm container of pad thai from her hands. It smells divine, and I realize I'm famished. I wheel the boys back to the café, with all our treasures from the farmer's market, pack everything into the car, and drive home.

I'm feeling a bit more hopeful after talking to Aranya. I'm still incredibly disappointed about what happened today with Phoebe, but at least it looks like I have help for the café, and I think Damien will be pleased as well.

Chapter 17

Damien shows up the next morning bright and early, and I know by now it's pointless to tell him that he should be at home. If he wants to be here cooking to take his mind off things, then who am I to argue?

"I have a bit of what I think you'll consider good news at least."

"Lay it on me. I need it," he tells me.

"I met Aranya Bunmi at the farmer's market last night."

"Oh yeah, from the food truck!"

"The one and only. What do you think of hiring her to help us out part-time?"

"Seriously? I think that would be fantastic! She's in culinary school too, so she can help me with some of the cooking. It would be good for her to learn the ropes in other ways, too, I would imagine."

"She's coming by at around 10:00 to talk some more, but even from our brief conversation last night, I really liked her, plus Marshall, Marcus, and Stumpy think she's the bee's knees."

"Did you get the pad thai?"

I laugh. Damien knows me so well. "I did, and it was fabulous. The spring rolls were amazing too."

"Hellloooo anyone home?" Gladys calls out from the front. Every day at precisely 6:30, she comes in for her breakfast burrito and coffee. She doesn't even have to order it; Damien just has it waiting for her.

This morning she's wearing a breezy cotton sundress with a large, brimmed straw hat and matching seashell-shaped purse. I would love to see her closet sometime. It must be enormous given all the different outfits and matching accessories she wears.

I take Glady's freshly prepared burrito and steaming cup of coffee out to her. "What's the news this morning?" I ask. Not that I really care that much about Crested Peaks gossip, but she often has the most interesting news to share.

She crooks her head in thought. "It's been somewhat quiet this week. I mean, aside from all the chatter about Cody, Darla, and Harold. No offense Damien!" she says as she notices him watching us from the kitchen doorway.

"None taken. I know it's on everyone's minds right now."

"Have you heard anything new about the case?" I query.

"Nothing beyond what I'm sure you're already aware of. Lots of speculation about Harold and Darla having an affair and Cody killing her out of anger, but no solid evidence of that from what I can tell. I didn't know Cody well, but I can't picture him killing someone. I guess lover's quarrels can bring out the worst in anyone."

Damien looks so sad it breaks my heart. "Gladys, I'm stating for the record, and you can tell it to anyone you want that I, Charlotte Duffin, don't believe for a second that Cody killed Darla."

She looks confused. "But why would he confess if he didn't do it? That's a horrific thing to confess to if you're innocent."

I shrug. "I don't know. I just have a feeling he didn't do it."

"Here's news you may not know. They hired a new guard at the prison."

"I have you there Gladys, because I do know that. Drew told me last night. But I don't know anything about him," I admit.

An all-knowing look crosses Gladys' face. "His name is Jerod Karr, and he worked as a security guard at the Denver Mint before moving up here. Although I haven't figured out yet why he left Denver, I'm working on it. Otherwise, that's all I know."

"Don't worry, I may be able to get more from Drew if you want," I reassure her.

"Yes, I'd appreciate that. You know I don't like to have incomplete information about anything."

"I am well aware of that," I laugh.

After that exchange, I let Gladys enjoy her breakfast in peace while I wait on other customers. Business is brisk, and I'm relieved when I remember that Aranya is coming in at 10:00 for an interview. I hope she can start work soon because we desperately need the help.

When Aranya shows up right on time, it's slow enough by then that Damien and I can sit down and talk to her at length about what kind of help we need at Marcall's. She, of course, brought treats for my pesky creatures, and they grab them from her hands and take off to enjoy them in the back office.

She agrees to start next week, after assuring me that her parents are fine with her coming to work here, as long as she can still help them out in the food truck when they need her.

Right after Aranya leaves, I insist that Damien go home. It looks like it will be a relatively quiet day, and I'm sure his family needs him far more than I do. I swear that if we're suddenly overrun with hungry customers, and I need his help, I'll call him so he can come back.

About 30 minutes after Damien leaves, I'm in the kitchen cleaning when I hear the door chime. "Hello! Welcome to Marcall's, what can I—oh, hi there!" It's Hilda Barnes. For a moment, I'm so thrown I almost don't know what to do.

"Hello!" she chirps. "After our conversation yesterday and hearing from all your raving fans for months, I decided I had to come check things out for myself!"

"Yes, of course, welcome!"

"This place is adorable," she says while looking around. "And you have rabbits!" she exclaims.

I look over to see that the rabbits have woken up from their nap and are in the dining area staring at Hilda.

"They belonged to my grandma."

"They're delightful! But why are their ears all crooked? Is something wrong with them?"

"No, they just came that way," I grin.

"I've never seen that on a rabbit!"

"They call them helicopter ears," I explain.

I watch Marshall tilt his head at her like he's trying to figure something out. "She's a witch," he tells me.

"What?" I respond out loud before I can catch myself.

"What?" Hilda says.

"Oh, uh, nothing." I shake my head. I have to be more careful about that.

I'm dying to ask Marshall if he's sure, and how would he know that, and I don't? Instead, I stare at him in a way that I hope gets my point across.

"She's a witch, and she's cloaking her powers. If you had more experience, you'd know that," he informs me.

"Oh, excuse me!" I retort.

"I'm sorry, what?" Hilda looks at me with growing concern.

I have got to stop doing that. This could quickly turn into a round of Who's On First if I'm not careful. "Please, pay no attention to my outbursts. I'm just talking to myself."

"Oh, well, I hear everyone talking about the Damien Special, so I think I'll take two of those to go!"

"Fabulous! I'm sure you'll love it," I tell her as I wrap up two burritos for takeout. The Damien Special is a highly guarded secret where even I don't know the details. It's a mixture of eggs, black beans, cheese, potatoes, grilled jalapenos, and caramelized onions, all layered with a secret sauce.

"It's a shame what happened to that boy, isn't it?" she tsks.

"What boy is that?" I ask, confused.

"That young man who killed Harold's assistant. But I'm glad he confessed. Now the rest of us don't have to worry about a murderer running loose in Crested Peaks. And her poor family won't have to endure a trial and all that."

"Yes, I suppose that's true," I murmur.

I suddenly have so many questions I want to ask her. Why is she hiding the fact she's a witch? Why did she say she was rehearsing with Harold when Darla was killed while Harold tells a different story? Does she know what Harold's secret is? Are they both in on it? I can't shake the feeling something is really off, and it's giving me the heebie-jeebies.

"Excuse me, Charlotte?"

"Yes?"

"Can I have some napkins?"

"Oh, yes, of course! Sorry about that," I tell her as I hastily stuff some napkins into the bag along with her burritos. I'm so lost in thought I completely zoned out. It's like there's something tiptoeing around the edge of my brain, and I'm on the verge of realizing what it is when it disappears again.

"Poor Harold has been so distraught over Darla's death, I'm hoping some pampering will cheer him up," she declares as she holds up her bag of burritos.

"I hope so! Let me know what you think of them."

After Hilda leaves, I feel nothing but unsettled. Even though I can't read her like I can Harold, this is one is solely based on my gut feeling. Something is just so off about her. At this point there isn't much I can do about it I suppose.

The funeral is tomorrow, and I plan to watch Harold and Hilda very carefully. I'm hoping that I can get a better read on Harold and armed with the new information about Hilda, I'll be studying her even closer from now on.

Chapter 18

Damien is covering for me at the café during the funeral. Although given all the buzz that Darla's murder has generated in this small town, I don't know if there will be anyone left to visit the café. They'll all be packed into the church.

He feels it wouldn't be the best idea to show up at the funeral for a person his own cousin confessed to killing. I told him that I could just close the café for the day so he could stay with his family, but he insisted it remain open.

Yet another reason to be happy about our new hire. It's kind of silly at this point to have just the two of us juggling everything.

Who could have imagined that I would be running a café that's so successful there's now three of us? Almost a year ago, I left New York broken-hearted and humiliated after being dumped by my fiancé to come to Colorado for a life I insisted I never wanted. And yet now, I couldn't imagine myself without it. Life is so weird sometimes.

Drew had to go to the station this morning, so I'll pick him up there on our way to the chapel. I've chosen a simple yet elegant black dress along with classic silver jewelry. My hair is jet black today. A far cry from the sweet and festive dress I had on two days ago when dinner was abruptly cut short.

I feel horrible thinking about Darla's life ending the way it did, and now Cody's too. I get chills thinking about the idea that he may not have killed her, which means an innocent man will go to prison for the rest of his life, and a murderer will go free.

But if I'm wrong, and Cody did kill Darla, then he should pay for that senseless act of violence. Part of me feels like maybe I'm just tilting at my own windmills. I was falsely accused of a crime, so now maybe I'm convinced Cody has been as well?

I leave the familiars at home and drive to the police station. But then I regret not bringing a lint roller when I notice the rabbit hair all over my black dress. You'd think that with talking rabbits the least they could do is warn me. Miranda helped me with a spell that keeps the café free from any unwanted pet hair and I'm thinking I should have done it at home as well.

As I stand outside the police station, unsuccessfully trying to brush white rabbit hair from my dress, it occurs to me that I can use magic to do it. As I start to focus on the hair leaving my dress, and falling to the ground, out of the corner of my eye I notice movement.

I pause my dress cleaning efforts and peer into the distance. Some-one is definitely moving around in the bushes lining the station wall. But why would they be crawling through the bushes at the police station? Because they're up to no good is my first thought.

I consider going over there to find out who it is, and see what they're up to when Hilda walks out of the hedges. I gasp out loud I'm so startled, and then she looks right at me. I can't think of anything to do other than wave at her, but she pretends not to see me as she backs up behind a tree.

What on earth? I start to approach her when Drew emerges from the station. "Hey Char, what are you staring at?" I jump I'm so startled. "I'm sorry," he says. "I didn't mean to sneak up on you."

I point to the tree where Hilda is hiding. "I just saw Hilda Barnes lurking in those hedges."

His brow wrinkles in concern. "Are you sure? Why would Hilda be in the bushes? She shouldn't be in there." He stares into the distance, but neither of us can see her. He turns back and looks at me like I must be making it up. "Where did she go?"

"She hid behind that tree when she realized I saw her."

"I better go check it out," he says as he walks toward the tree, and naturally, I start to follow, but then he pauses. "You stay put."

"Fine," I grumble as I pout and fold my arms over my chest in defiance. Drew confidently, yet ever watchful, strides to the tree I pointed out and walks around it. I wait with bated breath wondering what Hilda will do when Drew finds her. Instead, I'm shocked and a little disappointed, when he shakes his head and holds his hands up to indicate there's no one there.

"What?" I exclaim. "How can that be? I just saw her duck behind there!"

"She's gone now," Drew says.

"I swear I saw her sneaking around here as if she were someplace she shouldn't have been. Then she looked right at me but pretended not to see me when I waved."

"I believe you. The question is, what was she doing here? You know, a couple of days ago, a patrolman indicated the same thing, but it was late at night, so he thought the light may have been playing tricks on his eyes.

He swore that when he got closer, whatever it was, was gone. We asked him if it could have been a raccoon, and he said it appeared much bigger than that. More like a small person."

"What do we do now?" I ask.

"Now, we go to the funeral."

"Did you know that Hilda is a witch?" I ask him.

"Really? I didn't know that. Although I don't really know all of them, I'm sure you're more aware of that than I am."

"It's actually not even so much that she's a witch. It's that she's purposely hiding it that makes me suspicious."

"You can sense that?" Drew asks.

"Um." I hesitate.

Drew places his hands on his hips. "Let me guess. One of the rabbits told you."

"Marshall."

"I see."

"He said she's a witch who's cloaking her powers, so other Supernaturals don't know."

"Then how does he know this?" Drew asks, looking increasingly skeptical.

I shrug. "He said if I had more experience, I would know."

"What does Miranda say about this?"

"I haven't had a chance to ask her yet."

"But you're sure you can trust Marshall on this?" Drew persists.

"You have to remember, Gran had them for decades, which isn't normal for a rabbit, ever, so who knows what kind of talents they might have that they haven't told me about yet."

"There's no time to investigate any of this now, and if we don't hurry, we'll be late for the funeral."

"You look very distinguished, by the way," I tell him. He's wearing a navy-blue suit with a cream-colored shirt and a yellow tie with tiny blue polka dots. He's clean-shaven, and I swear he has a hint of gel in his very short hair, giving him a more sophisticated look than he typically has when he's out chasing down the bad guys.

He looks down at himself and blushes a bit. "Thanks. I just wish it was for a happier occasion."

"I can't believe we're going to a funeral for someone even younger than us."

He shakes his head sadly. "Murder knows no age boundaries."

"You're still investigating this, aren't you?" I ask.

"We have a confession, Char."

"I know, but—"

"--Sometimes the guilty party is the one you least want it to be. The bad guy isn't always someone you don't like."

I protest. "I just have this feeling I can't shake."

"I'm not even supposed to be spending resources on this anymore, but I'll make you a deal. If I happen to come across compelling evidence that shows Cody falsely confessed, I will take a look, how's that?"

"Okay." I guess it's about the best I can hope for at this point. "Don't forget about Hilda sneaking around police headquarters."

"When I get back, I'll let everyone know they should keep an eye out for any suspicious lurkers around the building. If she's spotted again, I'll question her."

When we arrive at the Mountain Chapel, I'm not surprised to see a of ton people streaming into the church. "I guess a well-publicized murder sure attracts the crowds." Reporters mill about, hoping to get reactions from grieving attendees, no doubt. I see Darla's family at the entrance greeting her friends as they file in for the service.

Her mother looks like she's still in shock, which I suppose she is. I heard a rumor that her father died recently, and that's when they moved back to Crested Peaks. What a blow for her mom to experience two deaths like that in a short period of time.

We pay our respects to Darla's mother and relatives and enter the chapel. There are flowers everywhere, but I'm guessing the display up front, which takes up several feet of space, and threatens to topple the stand they're on, belongs to Harold.

I scan the room looking for Harold or Hilda, but in the crowded area, it's hard to find them at first. Surely, they'll be here. At least Harold will come. Maybe Hilda is still busy lurking around in someone's bushes. When I finally locate them through the sea of people, I notice that Hilda is watching me, but quickly turns away when we make eye contact.

They're sitting where Harold can keep a close eye on his massive flower display. Although at the moment, he's sobbing into a handkerchief while Hilda glares at him. "There's Harold and Hilda!" I hiss in Drew's ear.

"Mmm hmm," he murmurs rather absentmindedly.

"I think we should keep an eye on them."

"Mmm hmm."

Sure, it may be bad form to spy on people, who I still consider possible suspects, at a funeral. Still, if I'm right about Cody, then there's a lot at stake here.

Soon the ushers urge people to take their seats. We squeeze into the back row, which I prefer, so I can watch what everyone else is doing. After most of the people are seated, Darla's family walks in.

Harold is still sobbing so loudly several people turn to see who's making all the noise. Some look at him like they pity him. Others look askance like he shouldn't be grieving that loudly, especially when most of them have undoubtedly heard the rumors about him and Darla.

The funeral is similar to most that I've been to with music and remembrance. But halfway through, Drew's phone must have buzzed in his pocket because he suddenly takes it out. When he looks at it, I know immediately the news is bad.

He shows me the screen, and I gasp so loudly several people turn to look.

Cody Murphy tried to poison himself. En route to hospital now.

Chapter 19

"Do you have to go?" I whisper. I can't believe this is happening.

"Yes, I think I should," Drew tells me as he lays a reassuring hand on my leg.

Cody must have tried to kill himself over the guilt. How could I have been so wrong about him? "I'll come with you," I tell him.

"Actually, I need you to stay here."

"What? Why? I won't interfere or anything. What if Damien needs me?" I beg.

"I'm sure Damien will be okay for now. He'll be busy, and I need you to be my eyes and ears here."

"Really?" is he seriously asking me to investigate the situation for him? "What's going on?" Suddenly I'm suspicious that he's not telling me everything.

Not once has he ever asked me to keep an eye on something. He knows something I don't. And that's not a witch's intuition. That's girlfriend intuition.

Drew texts back in rapid succession. He isn't letting me see what he writes, but I catch bits and pieces, and I swear he types something about having access to Cody.

"What if Damien needs to leave the café?" I suggest getting more worried by the moment.

"I'll send a patrol car by Marcall's to notify him of the situation if he doesn't already know. I'll tell him to lock up so the officer can escort him to the hospital. Will that work?"

"Yes, that's fine. Do you need my car?"

"No, my captain is coming to pick me up. Keep an eye on Hilda and Harold. If they leave, call me. But do not follow them, understand?"

"Now I know something is up here. Why is your captain picking you up? What's going on?"

"I'll explain everything when I have more answers. Just keep an eye on those two," he orders, nodding his head in their direction.

After Drew quietly slips out the back door, I glue my eyes to Harold and Hilda. Harold is still blubbering loudly into his handkerchief, but I notice that Hilda keeps looking down at her lap. Is she looking at her phone? What could be so important that she's fascinated by her phone in the middle of a funeral?

Once the service ends, I'm relieved to see the two of them file downstairs with the rest of the mourners to the lounge area for the reception. I was worried they would leave, and what else could I do but follow them? Even though Drew gave strict instructions not to.

First, Cody tries to kill himself, then Drew leaves in the middle of a funeral but insists I stay to watch Hilda and Harold. This whole thing gets weirder by the moment.

About 20 minutes or so into the reception, I get a text from Drew.

Cody expected to make a full recovery. Swallowed very little poison, fortunately.

Phew, there's that, at least. Although the sad truth remains that he still tried to poison himself, and even I have to admit it's looking more and more likely that he killed Darla.

I text back.

We're at the reception now. Hilda and Harold still here.

Good.

I maintain a watchful eye on them while trying not to appear like I'm stalking them. This is kind of exciting. Drew never gives me permission to be a sleuth, basically, I just do it and then ask for forgiveness later.

I'm so intent on keeping track of those two while I chew on my finger sandwich that the chapel has provided for lunch that I don't even notice when Miranda slides into the chair next to me.

"Whatcha doin?" she asks as I nearly jump out of my chair. "Whoa!" she says as she puts her hand on my arm to steady me. "Nervous much?"

"I'm supposed to keep track of Harold and Hilda. If they try to leave, I have to contact Drew right away."

"What? You're kidding me. What's going on? And why isn't Darla's mother here?"

I sigh in exasperation as I continue to stare at them. "I heard someone mention that they had to take her home right after the service because a doctor was going to give her a sedative; she was so upset. And don't tell anybody, but Cody tried to poison himself earlier today."

Miranda's eyes get huge. "Oh, no, that's horrible. Out of guilt over Darla?" she asks, almost like she's afraid to even say it out loud. "Is that why Drew left?"

"That's certainly what it looks like. But I saw something on Drew's text messages about having access to Cody at the police station. He also told me not to let Harold or Hilda out of my sight."

"This whole thing gets stranger and stranger."

I nod my head. "Doesn't it, though?"

"Hilda doesn't seem happy. She can't tear herself away from her phone while Harold can't stop crying," Miranda points out.

"It started right as Drew was leaving. Hilda has had her face buried in the phone ever since then. And Harold has been openly weeping the entire time."

Just then, Harold steers Hilda over into a corner. He keeps pushing her phone away as if he's encouraging her to stop texting. Hilda jerks her arm back so he can't touch her phone, and then they argue. Quietly at first, but it escalates quickly.

"Should we move closer so we can hear better?" I suggest

"Of course, we should!" Miranda replies.

Miranda and I try to move closer to the squabbling couple without attracting too much attention. Although we don't really have to worry, considering everyone else's attention is on the two of them arguing in the corner.

"You were having an affair with her right under my nose! You humiliated me! Did the two of you have a good laugh over the whole thing?" Hilda shrieks.

"Honey, I promise you, we weren't having an affair," Harold begs.

"How stupid do you think I am? I saw the bracelet you bought for her!"

Harold looks surprised. "That bracelet was for you."

"Then why was her name on the box?" she fires back.

He looks confused for a moment but then remembers. "Because I asked her to pick it up from the jewelers. I told them my assistant Darla would be picking it up and they obviously put her name on it."

"Oh, you liar! What kind of fool do you take me for?" she cries.

As I watch this scene play out before me, the sensation that Harold is lying only grows stronger, and when I finally realize what he's lying about, the energy coming from him is so intense it makes my head swim.

"You're her father!" I blurt out.

Hilda and Harold, who were unaware I was even standing nearby, both whip their heads around to look at me. Hilda, amid her hysteria, snarls at me, "He's not my father, you oaf."

"How did you know?" Harold whispers, his face turning pale as he realizes that someone has discovered his secret.

Then Hilda gets it. "Wait. You're Darla's father? That's impossible!"

He slumps onto a chair nearby. "We were 18," he begins softly. "I had no idea. If I had known, I would have married her in a heartbeat. I would have married her whether there was a baby or not. All I knew was that Laurel, her mother, just disappeared with her family one day without any explanation.

"Eventually, Laurel fell in love with someone else and married him. He raised Darla as his own. After he died last year, Laurel and Darla moved back to Crested Peaks. I did the math and confronted Laurel. She finally admitted that Darla was my daughter."

Harold continues his almost whispered confession. The entire reception hall is so silent that even his soft voice is heard by all. "I did what I could to take care of her without telling her who I really was. I gave her a job, tried to give her advice, encouraged her to make it on her own first. She was too young to be tied to a boyfriend. I didn't like him, but if I realized he was going to kill her, I would have done so much more to keep them apart."

Just then, Drew and several CPPD officers appear in the doorway, and every head in the reception hall swivels to their dramatic entry.

Drew's rich baritone voice echoes throughout the hall when he announces, "Hilda Barnes, you're under arrest for the attempted murder of Cody Murphy."

Chapter 20

Harold and I echo, "What?" while Hilda sprints for the emergency exit. For a second, I'm too stunned to even move. Then I realize Hilda is getting away. Drew and his men struggle to get through all the people and the chairs scattered throughout the area.

My heart hammering, I focus on the carpet runner beneath her feet. Just as Hilda nears the door, I focus every bit of energy I have on it and yank the carpet out from under her, sending her sprawling to the ground. For extra measure, I bolt the emergency door while I'm at it.

Miranda grins at me. "Nice job!"

As she lay spread eagle on the floor, Drew runs over to her, grabs her hands, and pulls them behind her back, pulling out his handcuffs and securing her. As he pulls her to her feet, she kicks and yells and struggles to get away.

"I'll hex every single one of you!" she screams as the crowd gasps and backs up out of fear. A couple of people even duck as if a hex could come zooming toward them at any moment.

Miranda and I, already on high alert, use a power-dampening spell on her to keep her from doing just that. It's a highly advanced skill, and I couldn't hold it for long on my own. But I know Miranda can.

"You're a witch?" Harold asks in shock.

I'm stunned. How could Harold not know his own girlfriend is a witch?

"Wait, did Drew just say she's under arrest for trying to kill Cody?" Miranda mutters to me out of the side of her mouth.

In all the commotion and shock that didn't register until just now. "He did!" I whisper back.

Against my better judgment, I approach her. But I know Miranda will cover me. "Charlotte, stay back," Drew warns. "She's in police custody now, and I'm taking her to the station to book her."

I hold up my hand to indicate I just need a moment. "This is why I saw you hiding in the bushes outside the police station? You were trying to kill Cody? But why?" Then it hits me. "Yesterday, you told me that it was a 'shame what happened to that boy,' and it seemed like a weird way to phrase it at the time, but I couldn't quite put my finger on why.

"Nothing had really happened to him – he just murdered Darla for all any of us were supposed to know – but you said that because you knew something was going to happen to him. You slipped up and spoke too soon."

Then an idea pops into my head that seems so utterly ludicrous I hesitate before saying it out loud. If I'm wrong, I'll really look like a lunatic. "Somehow, you framed him for Darla's murder, and then you had to get rid of him, so there wasn't anything to tie you back to him!"

The crowd gasps, and even Drew looks surprised by this. I admit it, I'm kind of just throwing out guesses here, but I think I'm at least close.

"You're all so stupid!" she snarls. "I killed Darla because I thought she was messing with my man, and nobody comes between me and my man!"

Harold is definitely looking a little green right now. Like he might throw up.

She boasts, "It all fell into place easier than I could have ever imagined when precious Darla turned down Cody's proposal."

"You were there that night?" I sputter.

"Yes, I was there that night!" she practically spits at me. And then she laughs a shrill, high maniacal laugh. Some people in the reception hall look uncomfortable as if they shouldn't be listening to this performance, and yet they can't seem to turn away.

"What night?" Harold asks. "Where?"

I turn to him. "Cody proposed to Darla at the Hotel Glacier on July 3rd, but she rejected him."

When Harold's mouth falls open in shock, I realize he didn't know either. For once, it seems like Crested Peaks managed to keep a secret.

Hilda continues, "After I came across the bracelet, I knew they were having an affair. Or at least I thought I did." At that, she almost shrugs apologetically. "And when she turned down Cody's proposal, I was convinced Harold was getting ready to leave me, and I had to do something fast."

She jerks her head at Harold. "I assumed with Darla out of the way and Cody convicted of her murder, that left you free and clear for me." Then she glares at him. "Why didn't you tell me? If only you'd been honest with me, I wouldn't have had to kill her!"

Harold looks like he can't believe he's actually hearing this. In a flash, he lunges at her and screams, "You killed my daughter!" He grabs at her and tries to shake her while Drew struggles to pull him off her and while keeping her detained.

The other officers leap into action to help Drew. It's sheer pandemonium, with the funeral attendees crying out in shock and dismay.

Once Hilda is hauled away in the squad car, Drew, Miranda, and I attempt to restore order. Drew tells everyone to sit down and remain calm. He doesn't want the crowd to rush out the door and drive away in a frenzy. I'm still numb over Hilda's confession.

"Try to get people calmed down if you can. Encourage them to stick around and eat. I have to get back to the station and sort things out," Drew tells us.

"Cody!" I exclaim. In all the chaos, I nearly forgot he's in the hospital. And he can go free now. "How did you know to arrest Hilda for trying to kill Cody?"

"Jerod Karr, the new guard, snuck the rat poison into Cody's food and then left the box for us to find so it would look like suicide. But he screwed up if you can call it that. He didn't give him enough to kill him. Just make him sick. The hospital already planned to keep him overnight for observation and then return him to lockup tomorrow. Obviously, I'll contact a judge and have him released from custody as soon as possible."

My jaw drops. "He was poisoned by the new prison guard? Why? I thought that's why Hilda was sneaking around the station. So she could kill him herself. A guard?" I ask a second time. I'm still so stunned to learn all of this. And confused.

"You're not the only one with instincts," Drew boasts. "When I learned that Cody had poisoned himself, my first thought was suicide. But then I couldn't get the idea of you seeing Hilda, hiding near the police station, out of my head. Add that to the fact you said she's a witch but keeping it a secret. So as much as I wanted to ignore your persistent theory that Cody wasn't guilty, it kept nagging me."

I place my hands on my hips and raise an eyebrow at him.

"I know, I know, you're right again," he admits.

"And that's when you told the station to hold Jerod." I clap my hands together triumphantly.

Drew sighs. I know it's hard for him to admit his witchy, café owning, girlfriend, who never attended a day of instruction at the Police Academy, just might be right about crime solving from time to time. "Yes. I knew if I was wrong, then I'd owe a huge apology to Jerod, and my fellow officers, in addition to being in big trouble with my captain. But if I was right—"

"—And me!" I proclaim, pointing at myself for emphasis.

"And you," he nods his head. "If we were right, then I had a killer to catch." This time he points at himself for emphasis. "However, what I didn't know, at the time, was why. Fortunately for us, upon questioning, Jerod cracked quickly.

"Hilda dug up some damning information on him and used it to blackmail him. She convinced him to poison Cody and set it up to make it look like suicide over his guilt about killing Darla.

"He swears he didn't know why Hilda would want to kill Cody, however. And Cody's own confession was still on the table, so at that point, I still had no reason to think that anyone but Cody had killed Darla."

I shake my head in wonderment. "I still can't believe this has all happened. I never really thought that Cody killed Darla, but I just assumed it could easily be Harold because I knew he was covering up a huge lie. Not once did it occur to me that they were related."

"I really have to get back to the station now, but I'll update you when I have new information. Oh, and Damien is at the hospital right now with Cody if you want to fill him in."

"Damien!" I yelp. I forgot about him too. I'm a horrible friend. This day has been so wild I don't seem to know which way is up.

"Are you okay to drive yourself to the hospital, or do you want me to drop you off?" Drew asks.

"I'm fine. I'll grab Miranda, and we'll head over there. He'll be so relieved."

After Drew leaves for the police station, Miranda and I drive in the opposite direction toward the hospital. We almost don't know what to say to each other we're still in shock. "Just like that, Hilda confesses. I still can't believe it. I always considered her a suspect, but I didn't expect her to just confess like that. And at one point, I thought Phoebe was off her rocker too. But Hilda basically said, 'hold my beer.' And I still don't get why Cody confessed."

"She probably hexed him," Miranda explains.

"Into believing he committed murder?" I bluster. "That's horrible!"

"She may have found out about his past, and after Darla turned him down, it would have been relatively easy to convince him, using the right spell, that he blacked out."

"Obviously, it's bad enough that she murdered Darla to start with but then convinced another person they did it by using magic to manipulate them with their past. That's the worst thing ever. That's something my parents might have done." I'm so angry right now I could scream.

Miranda shakes her head in disgust. "Just like there are bad Non Supernaturals, there are obviously bad Supernaturals. Witches and wizards and all sorts of other magical types can use their magic to do evil. It sucks, but thanks to you and Drew, the real killer will be punished, and an innocent man goes free."

"Damien is going to be so excited! I can't wait to tell him."

Chapter 21

We almost got kicked out of Cody's hospital room for our boister-ous celebration; but now it's 10 PM and when we're driving back to Marcall's where Damien and Drew will join us.

While Damien and I wait in the dining area for Drew, Miranda prepares a celebratory tea. She won't tell us what's in it, but she assures us that it's extra healthy and will help mitigate the effects of all our celebrating tomorrow morning.

"Hey, Miranda!" Damien calls back to her.

"Yeah?"

"There's a platter of donuts in the refrigerator that we've been working on. Bring those out too, would you?"

"Roger dodger!" she replies.

"Do you think they're ready?" I ask. "I'm so excited!"

"I'm not ready to share them with customers yet, but I want to know what Miranda and Drew think," Damien explains.

It seems like we've been working on this new recipe forever, so I'm eager to test them out too. Damien is often secretive about his special dishes, and now we both of us get to share a secret recipe. And yes, this time, I'll admit that there's a little magic involved.

When Drew finally arrives, Damien, Miranda, and I are gathered around a table with our tea and the untouched donuts because Damien won't let anyone at them until we're all here.

Drew insisted we all get together at the same time so he doesn't have to tell the story more than once. He plunks himself down onto a chair and breathes a sigh of relief.

"Busy day?" I joke.

Miranda shoves a glass of tea at him, which he gulps down greedily.

"After spending the afternoon interrogating Hilda, we got quite a bit of information from her, at least before her lawyer petitioned a judge to have her admitted to a psychiatric hospital."

"Do you think she'll be admitted?" I ask. "She's clearly unstable, but I hate the thought of her just sitting in a hospital somewhere when she should be in jail!"

"Given what she and Jerod both admitted to. And the evidence we have against her, that contradicts Cody's confession, no matter where she ends up; she'll be locked up for a very long time," Drew patiently explains.

"Wait, what kind of evidence do you have that showed Cody was innocent? You never told me about this," I interject.

"I didn't say innocent," Drew continues. "I just said it contradicted his confession. But I have to admit it was one of the first things that gave me pause." Drew glances down at the donuts, probably wondering why we aren't eating them.

"Not yet," Damien says.

Drew shrugs and continues. "Remember when you two called me and asked me to use my CPPD authority to prevent a bus from leaving the station?"

Uh oh. Miranda and I nod slowly.

"My captain was giving me the high sign, while I was on the phone with you, that he had urgent news for me."

Even though I sweat a little, hoping that he doesn't know we actually stopped that bus, I add, "I remember that! You had to cut our conversation short because you said your captain wanted to talk to you."

"Precisely," he responds. And then, just as I think I might be off the hook, he adds, "And don't think I don't know about what you did to the bus, but we'll discuss that later." Miranda and I exchange guilty looks. Shoot. I thought we were getting away with that one.

"But as I was saying. When my captain interrupted the phone call, he wanted me to know that the fingerprint evidence from the vodka bottles, that we found in the dumpster at Cody's condo, didn't match Cody's prints.

"Couldn't he have dumped them elsewhere?" Miranda suggests only to endure a harsh look from Damien.

"What?" she asks. "I'm just sayin."

"Yes," Drew says. "He could have dumped the bottles somewhere other than the condo trash bin, but it seemed unlikely. Once they went in the trash, one would think that they could belong to anybody unless you dusted them for prints like we did.

"And if he had blacked out like he thought, it seems even less likely he'd think to throw them in the trash somewhere else. And before you ask," he says when he sees me ready to point something out, "I know that I told you he could have dumped the bloody clothes elsewhere. And I get that it seems contradictory. But most cases have elements that don't always make sense. But it lingered in my thoughts – no liquor bottles and no bloody clothes."

"And yet you still took Cody at his word when he confessed," Damien points out.

"We had a suspect, whose fingerprints were all over the weapon that belonged to him, who confessed to the murder. There wasn't a lot to investigate. Not at the time anyway.

"But thanks in part to my lingering uneasiness and Charlotte's persistence," I sit up tall and grin at this while Damien pats me on the back, "I couldn't quite let it go. And, as I told Charlotte earlier. The combination of Hilda getting caught hiding in the hedges, in front of the police station, plus Cody's sudden, alleged suicide attempt. I knew it was time to examine my hunch."

"And I already filled these two in on what you told me about the guard confessing to poisoning Cody," I add.

Drew nods. "After we got Hilda back to the police station, she bragged about hexing Cody. It was Hilda, who the patrolman saw at night, lurking in the hedges.

"When she thought that Harold and Darla were involved, she researched Cody's background. She had planned to approach him and let him know that his girlfriend was seeing her boss."

"Why didn't she?" I interrupt. Drew is taking his sweet time explaining this, and I'm getting antsy.

He holds a finger up to try and slow me down. "But when she came across what she thought was the bracelet Harold had bought for Darla, she decided to step it up a notch. And when Darla turned down Cody's proposal, it created the perfect storm."

"Holy smokes!" Miranda exclaims. "This is just bizarre!"

"Truth is sometimes stranger than fiction, right?" Drew adds. "Hilda used Cody's dagger knowing that we'd find his fingerprints all over it, and then eventually used witchcraft to provoke a confession from him. You two can probably explain this better than I can." Drew says as he gestures to the two of us.

I look to Miranda, knowing that she'll have more answers than me. She takes a deep breath. "As you can imagine, something like that requires powerful magic. And it's considered taboo by the Supernatural Council. The governing body for Supernatural beings," she explains when she sees the confused looks on Drew and Damien's faces.

"Obviously, to use that kind of magic to trick someone into confessing to a crime that you committed, murder no less, is heinous. One of the worst things you could do to a person. Aside from the actual murder, of course.

"It's a difficult spell to maintain. Hilda would have had to keep adding energy to the spell, which I would guess is also why she knew she had to get rid of Cody eventually. Once he went to the County Jail, she'd lose easy access, his true memory would come back, and he'd insist he didn't do it after all."

"Although even that wouldn't have guaranteed he could go free," I shudder. "It would just be him recanting his confession without proof he was innocent."

"Yes, but Hilda decided even that risk was too great and blackmailed Jerod, the new guard, into poisoning Cody for her," Drew explains.

"This whole thing is like one of those episodes you see on a tv cop show, isn't it? What on earth could have been so severe you could blackmail someone into committing murder?" Damien asks shock registering on his face and in his voice. "And how would Hilda have known about it? Didn't you say Jerod was brand new?"

Drew sighs. "It seems our friend Hilda has a penchant for digging up dirt on people. She learned that Jerod was fired from his previous job as a security guard for stealing money from the Denver Mint."

At this, I giggle, prompting everyone to turn to me in surprise. "I'm sorry," I still laugh. "But Gladys had the part about the Denver Mint right, but now I'll get to give her the tea for once." The three of them still look at me, confused. I wave my hand through the air. "Never mind, I guess you had to be there."

Miranda asks, "How did he get hired with CPPD with a theft record?"

Drew jumps back in. "He has a hacker friend who falsified his records. A friend, who I might add, that now has an arrest warrant out for himself."

"But why wasn't Jerod arrested in Denver after they fired him for stealing?" I ask. I don't understand why this guy was free to try and kill Cody.

"Wow, you guys are quite the interrogators," Drew admits. The three of us smile at each other. "But don't get any ideas! Don't forget I still know about the bus."

"What's this about a bus?" Damien asks, as Miranda and I pretend not to hear the question.

"The Feds felt that, while there was enough evidence to fire him, there wasn't enough to prosecute him. As you can imagine, though, they are re-opening the case as we speak, and he's been charged with attempted murder and tampering with a prisoner here in Crested Peaks. Our guard is in a lot of trouble."

"But wait," I suddenly remember. "If Cody didn't kill Darla, and it wasn't until after he was arrested that Hilda hexed him, why did he make up the false alibi to begin with? When there was no reason to lie in the first place."

Damien raises his hand. "This one I can answer. After Cody re-gained consciousness today, he told me that once he learned it was his dagger, he knew how bad it looked for him. Especially after Darla rejected his marriage proposal. And that they argued in public the next day about their relationship.

"He honestly didn't think the CPPD would catch him in the lie, they would find the real killer, and his story would go unnoticed. Once he got arrested, he realized he was in too deep and continued the lie."

"So, what was he doing the morning of the 4th?" I ask.

"Oh, he was installing the garbage disposal. That much was true. He just thought he'd embellish the story by saying he'd gone to the store that day too. If he'd just left that part out, at least it wouldn't have looked like he lied to the cops because he was guilty."

Silence falls over the four of us as we each ponder what a wild week this has been.

"I have to ask. What is the deal with these donuts?" Drew demands, breaking the silence. "Are they just here to mock us? They look delicious, why can't we have one?"

"Well?" I look over at Damien. "Are we ready?"

"All right, all right, try them and let us know what you think," Damien finally caves, removing the plastic wrap from the donut platter. Drew and Miranda each snatch one off the plate and take a huge bite. If it's a Damien creation, they know it's good. No need to be cautious.

"Damien!" Drew exclaims. "You've outdone yourself. I swear this is the best donut I've ever had."

"No need to exaggerate on my account," Damien responds.

Miranda shakes her head vigorously. "He's not exaggerating. This is heavenly. But it must be like ten zillion calories, amiright?"

I smile as I take the opportunity to stuff a bite of one in my own mouth.

"That may be the best part." Damien smiles proudly. "Thanks to a secret combination of already delicious ingredients from me, and" he nods in my direction, "a little witchcraft, these are actually half the calories of a regular donut."

"Whoa! No way!" Miranda exclaims. "Marcall's will be famous."

"We'll need a steady supply at the station," Drew says as he reaches for a second one. "Being cops and all."

Damien's mouth drops in shock. "Are you supposed to joke about that?"

Drew laughs. "I'm a cop. It's allowed."

"Damien and I have more news to share!" After the week we've had, Miranda and Drew almost look like they're afraid of what I might say. "Marcall's has officially hired another employee!"

Miranda squeals. "No way! Do we know them?"

"Aranya Bunmi from the Thai One On food truck."

"Oh, that's fantastic!" she says.

Drew's face breaks into a huge smile. "You really hired someone. Why didn't you tell me?"

"In all the drama otherwise, I almost forgot about it. And when I did remember, it didn't quite seem appropriate to bring up, given everything else that was going on. Especially since it involved Damien's family." I explain.

"That's fantastic news! I'm happy for both of you, and this calls for a celebration. Why don't we all meet for dinner tomorrow night at the Hotel Glacier?" Drew suggests.

"I'm in! I'll see if Miles is free," Miranda responds.

"Us too!" says Damien.

I glance over at Drew. "Looks like we'll get our dinner out this week after all."

He smiles. "I guess we will."

As I watch Damien, Drew, and Miranda all talking and laughing about the future, I get goosebumps realizing how amazing it is to finally have a real family. I wish Gran were here to enjoy all of this too, but I'm sure she's watching us from up above and smiling. No doubt she's happy she's the one who put all of this in motion in the first place.

Thank You!

Note: This is a work of fiction. Names, characters, places, and incidents are a product of the author's imagination. Locales and public names are sometimes used for atmospheric purposes. Any resemblance to actual people, living or dead, or to businesses, companies, events, institutions, or locales is completely coincidental.

9 798201 045081